Sherlock Holmes
The Disappearance of Henry Fyldene

A Resurgent Mystery

J. B. Varney

Copyright © 2023 J. B. Varney

All rights reserved.

ISBN: 9798854095471

DEDICATION

To the memory of

Jeremy Brett

who brought Holmes to life
for millions of fans
1933-1995

"The game is... still afoot!"

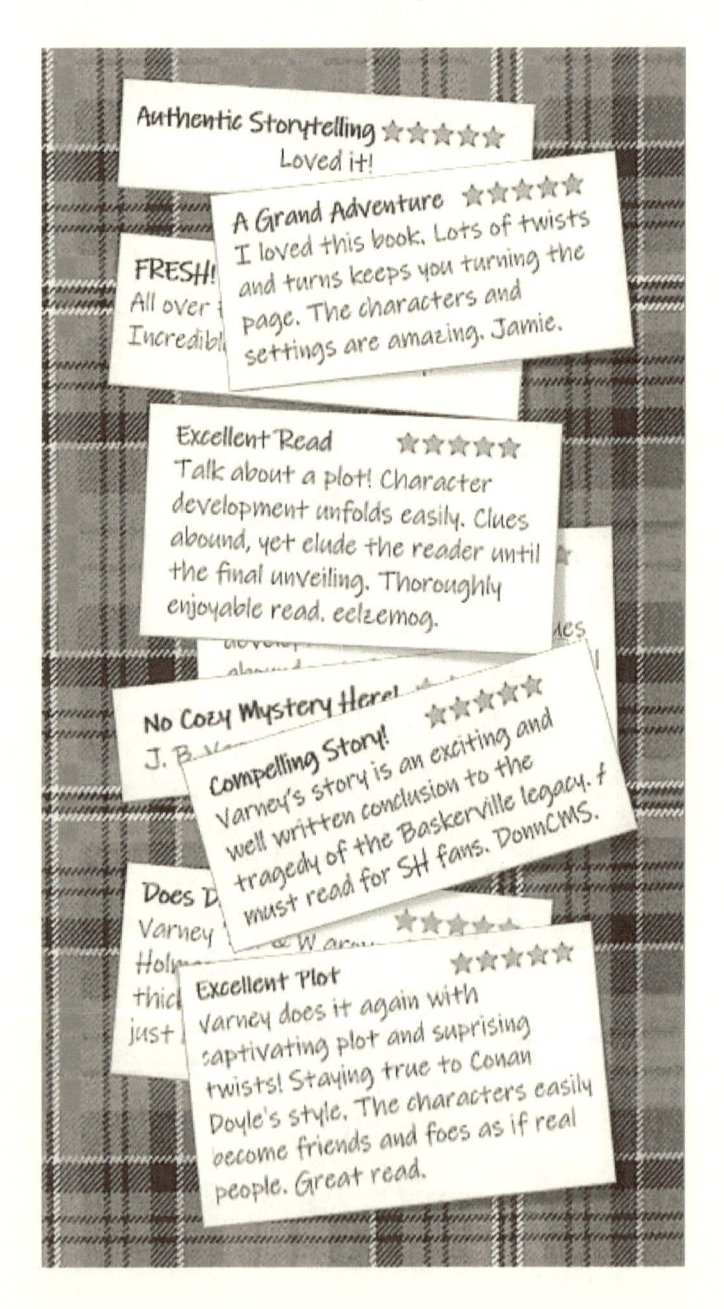

J. B. Varney

Authentic Storytelling ★★★★★
Loved it!

A Grand Adventure ★★★★★
I loved this book. Lots of twists and turns keeps you turning the page. The characters and settings are amazing. Jamie.

FRESH!
All over
Incredibl

Excellent Read ★★★★★
Talk about a plot! Character development unfolds easily. Clues abound, yet elude the reader until the final unveiling. Thoroughly enjoyable read. eelzemog.

No Cozy Mystery Here! ★★★★★
J. B.

Compelling Story! ★★★★★
Varney's story is an exciting and well written conclusion to the tragedy of the Baskerville legacy. A must read for SH fans. DonnCMS.

Does D
Varney
Holm
thic
just

Excellent Plot ★★★★★
Varney does it again with captivating plot and suprising twists! Staying true to Conan Doyle's style. The characters easily become friends and foes as if real people. Great read.

The Sherlock Holmes Resurgent Mystery Series

Book 10

"The game is... still afoot."

Burke's Peerage speaks of Sir Richard Osborne and Elizabeth Fyldene marrying at Ashford in Kent in 1511. Mr. Varney is their 14th Great-Grandson. Other descendants include a Lord Mayor of London and the 1st Duke of Leeds. The latter being one of "The Immortal Seven," who offered the crown to William III.

Mr. Varney is the 15th Great-Grandson of Robert Broughton (died 1506) Knight and Member of Parliament. Sir Robert was knighted at the Battle of Stoke, where he fought on the Lancastrian side under John de Vere, 13th Earl of Oxford. He married the Earl's daughter, Katherine.

Contents

Chapter 1 – The Indomitable Lady 1

Chapter 2 – The Fog 18

Chapter 3 – Granby Street 39

Chapter 4 – Mrs. Fyldene's Secret 61

Chapter 5 – The House of Blood & Death 79

Chapter 6 – The Consulting Detective 97

Chapter 7 – The Stars Align 122

Chapter 8 – The Dead Diplomats 140

Chapter 9 – The Hour Grows Late 159

Chapter 10 – The Hermitage 175

Chapter 11 – The Dying Chieftain 192

Chapter 12 – Darlington 211

Henry Fyldene

Chapter 1 – The Indomitable Lady

In the year 1878 I took my degree of Doctor of Medicine from the University of London and went on to Netley to go through the course prescribed for surgeons in the army.[1] Having successfully passed my studies I was duly attached to the 5th Northumberland Fusiliers as an Assistant Surgeon. Upon my arrival in India and in the manner so common to the Army in those days, I was then transferred to the 66th Royal Berkshires with whom I served at the ill-fated battle of Maiwand in the Afghan in July of 1880.

Wounded and sick, having contracted enteric fever, that curse of our Indian possessions, I was dispatched to England with a few hundred other lads, all in a similar condition, on the troopship Orontes. A month or so later we landed at Portsmouth, my health still a matter for concern to my physician. I was ordered to recuperate, so far as was possible upon an income of eleven shillings sixpence per day. It was in these straits that I was laid hold upon in the Criterion Bar by an old friend, Stamford, who had been a dresser at St. Bartholomew's Hospital when I was finishing my degree.[2]

---

[1] Netley was the site of the Royal Victoria Military Hospital and is often simply referred to simply as "Netley."
[2] Dresser – a newly graduated doctor.

We lunched at the Holborn, a last splurge upon my eleven shillings sixpence, and I poured out my sorrows upon the poor chap. I bemoaned the fact that I must now abandon London, with all its distractions, for a quiet country seat where my existence, dull though it would be, would be had for a fraction of the cost. It was then that Stamford told me of an excellent opportunity to remain in London despite the expense, by halving my costs while doubling my comfort. It seemed too good to be true but I was desperate.

It was in 1881 that I first heard the name of Sherlock Holmes and despite Stamford's warnings regarding the man's *eccentricities*, in short order I was a resident of 221B Baker Street.

Thus I became Holmes' companion upon the adventures which would shape my life and, in time, I became his biographer and friend as well.

By 1884 I'd been with Holmes long enough to have laid down the foundations my system for tracking and recording our cases. Since that time I've maintained my notes and journals with few changes to that original system.

In that year several interesting cases came our way, but none were quite as recherché or exotic as the well-publicized disappearance of one of London's most eligible young beau's, Mr. Henry Fyldene, who was designated by the use of the archaic title of "the Younger." The papers had made much over the past weeks, of such things as his rowing career at Oxford, where he was one of the champion boys of '82 when they defeated Cambridge in the rowing-eight by seven lengths.

I'd witnessed that race from the Surrey-side of the Thames on a fine warm day with a breeze out of the north-west, although I could not then have told you which of the lads might have been the young Fyldene scion.[3]

The press had also made much of the fact that the young man's father, Henry Fyldene, the Elder, had spent a long career in the Diplomatic Corp, mostly in distant India or Ottoman Arabia.

What connection any of these things may have had to the disappearance of the young man was not noted in the papers and they continued to carry additional stories for weeks as Scotland Yard tried to bring it to a successful conclusion. The articles remained of the sensational sort and appeared to me to be of little actual significance at all to the case. As Holmes had not been sought out, however, it remained an academic matter.

To the sensational news I had but little further knowledge to add. I knew the Fyldene's were an ancient family, of course, with deep Norman roots and a sterling reputation for courage in battle. One of them, a James Fyldene, had served notably in the Afghan although he'd been killed by a sniper shortly after Maiwand.

---

[3] The Surrey-Side is the south side of the Thames, while the north side is referred to as the Middlesex-Side.

It was even rumored that the family could trace thirteen lines back to the first Viking Duke of Normandy, Rollo or Ganger Rolf.[4] This then was all I knew before our bell at 221B rang at half-ten on a cold, gusty November day.

I was rereading an article on the mammoths of Siberia by Sir Henry Howorth in one of my copies of the Geological Magazine to which I subscribed.[5] Holmes was engaged in some abstruse chemical experiment.

Neither of us was expecting anyone on such a day so when our page boy, Billy, came hurrying in with a lady's card of gold foil upon parchment stock we were both surprised.

"Mrs. Henry Fyldene, Ashburn House, Number 12 Park Street," Holmes read aloud.

"An excellent address," said I.

"No doubt the mother of the missing Oxford champion-rower," he observed.

He emptied his old rosewood pipe upon the grate and motioned to Billy to show her up. By habit we stood to greet Mrs. Fyldene, but there are times in life when nothing one has heard prepares one for the actual moment. This was one such time for me.

---

[4] Ganger Rolf – Rolf the Walker. It was said that the Viking warlord was too large for a horse to carry. It is more likely that the horses of the time could not carry him in his full battle dress and weapons. The war horses or destriers were bred larger and larger over the centuries which followed.

[5] Sir Henry Howorth, The Geological Magazine, Nov. 1880.

Henry Fyldene

If the card had read "Duchess" or "Princess of such and such," then we might have at least been more prepared for the beautiful and elegant lady who graced our humble sitting room that day.

As it was the name "Mrs. Henry Fyldene" did little to prepare us for our encounter.

"Gentlemen," she said, as she handed me her things, "thank you for allowing me this meeting."

Though the term is too often used I considered her to be a woman of breathtaking beauty, despite the sadness apparent in her eyes. The blossom of her skin and the brightness of her smile seemed that of a young woman instead of the mother of a grown man. She was regal yet with that rare combination of both kindness and confidence. When Shakespeare put the words in Hamlet's mouth, "Frailty, thy name is woman!" he most certainly had not had this woman in mind.

Her son's great physical strength had pulled the Oxford Eight to a victory in "The Boat Race of 1882," but I was impressed to see a different kind of strength from the woman seated before us.[6]

After seeing our guest to a seat and pouring out a cup of tea, Holmes took his chair opposite and invited Mrs. Fyldene to tell us the purpose of her visit. That she had come to seek our help in finding her son was logical, but my friend was that kind of man who, by principle, would assume nothing.

"Please take your time, but leave nothing out," Holmes said, "for the smallest point may be of immense importance."

"As you have no doubt read in the papers my husband chose to work through Scotland Yard toward the recovery of *our* missing son."

---

[6] The event, the third consecutive victory for Oxford, was of such moment that the name given it, "The Boat Race of 1882," was bestowed without any fear that it might be confused with any other boat race of any kind for that year.

She paused here for a moment and sipped at her tea.

"But I am concerned Mr. Holmes."

"Concerned, but why?" he enquired. Then, quickly deducing the reason, he said, "There have been no leads at all?"

The papers had been silent upon this point and Holmes had thrown them aside more than once in disgust at their uselessness.

"There have not," said she. "You have guessed our terrible secret Mr. Holmes."

Holmes stared in surprise as he'd expected the case to be fairly straightforward and resolved by the police within the span of a few weeks at most. Such disappearances, though they could hardly be said to be commonplace at that time, were sadly not altogether unheard of either and invariably ended in heartbreak for the families involved.

"I never guess Mrs. Fyldene," Holmes replied. I assure you."

"Well there have been no leads of any kind. In fact, nothing at all has been accomplished by the police as far as I can tell," she offered.

"And you have heard nothing directly?"

"Not a word from my son either Mr. Holmes. Nothing to tell me what might have befallen him."

"Is he prone to such thoughtlessness?" Holmes asked, choosing his words carefully.

"He has never once done anything like this but is always most conscious of my concerns."

"He is a popular young man is he not, if the papers may be trusted upon the subject?"

"He is and he has many friends in London with whom he regularly meets."

"And young men may be apt to fall in love..."

"Henry is not immune to such feelings and has, I believe, marked out one young woman more than the others. But she assures me that she has not heard a word from him either and is quite as worried as I am."

"You've twice spoken of your son in a way which excludes your husband Mrs. Fyldene."

"I don't understand," she replied.

"First you said that the young man was quite conscious of *your concerns,* then you remarked that the young woman was as worried as *you were*. At no time did you even hint that your son would not want to worry his father or disturb his plans. Is there some reason for this oversight? I must ask if there is more to this than you have revealed to us."

"You are indeed discerning Mr. Holmes and I'm sorry to say that my son's adolescence placed a great strain upon their relationship."

"And this *strain* you mentioned, are there other reasons for it beyond simple adolescence?"

The woman's hesitation before confirming her reasons gave me pause to wonder if Holmes had indeed seen or sensed something. Mrs. Fyldene seemed straightforward to me.

Holmes, however, possessed an eerie ability to see the invisible and the hidden, even behind a façade of deception.

"Would that explain why Mr. Fyldene has not accompanied you today?"

Holmes questions were again upon their mark.

"I was hoping you would not bring that up Sir, for it casts my husband in a poor light and one which is also...quite hurtful *to you* Mr. Holmes."

"Then he looks upon me in a *dubious light*?"

"That's a decidedly delicate way of expressing it Sir and it does you credit, but I'm afraid there is more to it than that."

"Please explain Mrs. Fyldene."

"Henry has no appellations or titles to affix to his name, but he is one of the Fyldene's of Kent, who are no mean people.[7] He clings to the old ways in many things and especially in the import they continue to grant to his family's standing. He is most emphatic in many of his beliefs and one in particular is that the only place for *amateurs*...is in sport. I beg your pardon for using the word in reference to you Mr. Holmes."

"So he believes if I am proficient at my trade I should prove it by being a professional, one of the fellows at Scotland Yard for instance?"

"I'm afraid that's very much it," she admitted.

---

[7] "mean" – used in the Victorian sense means insignificant or unimportant. To say, "they are no mean people," is to imply that they are a significant family.

"So he entrusts his son to the official forces?"

"If I may summarize his feelings, he sees your refusal to earn your living professionally to be the result of arrogance, the act...of an *upstart* in fact. Again, I must apologize."

"Please don't trouble yourself," Holmes said, graciously. "Have we not heard a great many such criticisms long before this Watson?"

"Indeed we have Mrs. Fyldene," I soothed, "in fact, Holmes is quite used to such reproaches. As you can see however, he disproves the doubters upon an almost daily basis."

"Which is precisely why I've come Dr. Watson. Your articles in the press are frequent reminders and solid proof of Mr. Holmes' ingenuity and effectiveness. I tend to be more open-minded than my husband, however, I am not always free to do as I wish. With the police so obviously frustrated in their investigation, I could wait no longer."

"You are an Osborne of Darlington are you not Mrs. Fyldene?" Holmes enquired.

The attractive woman looked at my friend with a penetrating gaze for a long moment.

"I don't assert my antecedents Mr. Holmes."

"A wise if unnecessary sacrifice for a woman of superior birth and connections, who finds herself married to an insecure man, frightened of nothing more than that his inferiority might be found out by the world at large."

Henry Fyldene

"I would be tempted to believe you know my husband Mr. Holmes, if I didn't already know that the exact opposite were true, but you must forgive my curiosity in asking how you came by your hard-won knowledge."

"My name is Sherlock Holmes," said he, boldly, "and despite your husband's *views* on my status as an amateur, it is my job to know the things which others do not."

"It's true, he suffers from insecurity, although I'd never say so much beyond these walls."

"This has no doubt added to the challenges of your marriage," said he.

"Many families strive to *marry up* Mr. Holmes, as they call it. The Fyldene's were no different and I was considered a good catch for their son, but our marriage has shown both of us the pitfalls of that practice."

"How so Mrs. Fyldene?" I asked.

"For one Dr. Watson, the Fyldene's in general and my husband, specifically, feel much freer to show their emotions and voice opinions than we do. You may doubtless imagine that such a trait was a welcomed blessing during courtship, for a young woman who had long doubted both her beauty and worth. What lady, after all, does not like to be reminded that the stars cannot compare with her beauty or that her eyes really are like shimmering azure pools?"

"Shimmering azure pools," Holmes whispered.

"It is true that no lady wants to be in doubt of her partner's ardor," said I, as I recalled my own experiences with the fair sex, limited as they were.

"Yet at Darlington we don't have the liberty of casual opinions and emotions are those things which are to be controlled, at all costs. Such things were considered uncouth and unacceptable. For another, while 'tis human to compare no doubt, by marrying me my poor Henry placed himself in the sad position where he could never achieve or acquire enough to feel secure in himself. He has been doomed to a kind of purgatory all these years and, despite his limitations, I do not believe him a bad man. His career was not notable, but even his accomplishments were easily overlooked as they paled next to those of many of his older peers. Whatever he did it was never deemed worthy of garnering him the attention, titles, and promotions which went so easily many of the men who'd been longer in the diplomatic corp."

"You speak of Sir Henry Rawlinson?" I asked.[8]

"It may be that I do Doctor," said she. "The Baronet certainly enjoyed an unusual degree of good will from the hierarchy."

"Some say the Baronet earned his place."

---

[8] Sir Henry Rawlinson, 1st Baronet Rawlinson, as a fledgling diplomat he came to the attention of his superiors in England and was made a Companion of the Order of the Bath in 1844, elected a Fellow of the Royal Society in 1850, and given the distinction of Knight Commander of the Order of the Bath shortly thereafter.

"And perhaps he did Dr. Watson, at least a portion of it at least, but Henry was hindered by haunting thoughts."

"Haunting thoughts?" Holmes asked.

"My husband was well aware of the fact that, while men like Henry Rawlinson received every preference in the field, back in England they were simply not the equals of the Fyldene's. They would not have had a place in their society and if they met in passing the place of each man would be acknowledged. Henry simply couldn't let go of such considerations."

The lady wore a pained look after this comment and I asked what it was that bothered her.

"I dislike speaking in such terms Dr. Watson, but I'm afraid there are still a great many, like my Henry, who measure a person's worth almost solely by their placement in Burke's Peerage."[9]

"I'm afraid it is the prevailing view for the vast majority of our fellow citizens," I offered, soberly.

"No doubt you are right Dr. Watson."

"To return to the subject," Holmes said, "what do you believe has happened to your son Mrs. Fyldene? After all, a mother is generally closer to her children than the father, is she not?"

"Like you Mr. Holmes, I suspected it might have had something to do with Miss Waldron."

---

[9] Burke's Peerage, Baronetage & Knightage, first published in 1826, records the ancestry and heraldry of the titled families of Great Britain and Ireland.

"The young woman you referred to earlier?"

"That's correct Sir."

"Even steady young men have been known to *falter* when faced with love," I offered.

"And I suspected as much Dr. Watson, mainly because that was the only reason I could imagine for which my son might *falter*, as you put it."

"But Miss Waldron allayed your suspicions?"

"Yes Mr. Holmes, Marianne assured me that she was as concerned by Henry's disappearance as was I, and as ignorant of its cause as well. I'm afraid that the Inspectors from Scotland Yard were extremely hard upon that poor girl."

"Do you recall their names?" Holmes enquired.

"The leader was a Mr. Gregson."

"And the other?"

"Redfern, Redman, or Redford perhaps."

"We know the men," I remarked, with a nod.

"I believe I understand the job the Inspectors have been tasked with well enough Doctor," she said, clearly upset. "I am young Henry's mother after all, but I see no excuse for the bullying of a seventeen-year-old girl Mr. Holmes, and one of the sweetest you'll ever meet. Their manner of handling me was bad enough, but I've at least seen the broader world and know how things can sometimes work out. A girl like Marianne though, she has no experience with any of that to guide her through such a terrifying ordeal."

"I am afraid Gregson can unfeeling," I agreed.

"Then you know the man?" she asked.

"Yes," Holmes replied, quietly, "and though it may disappoint you to hear it Mrs. Fyldene, the Inspector is among the better of Scotland Yard's pack of professional detectives. No doubt your husband would approve of him."

"For all Gregson's shortcomings," I said, "I can attest to the man's unwavering courage."

"And the other man?" she asked.

"A Mr. Launcelott Redgrave, a newcomer and recent addition from York I believe," I said.

"Well they should be ashamed of themselves."

"Does your son still live with you at Ashburn House," Holmes asked, looking at her card.

"He has rooms there and always shall, but he stays elsewhere when he is in London. During his college days he was obviously often away."

"I would like to see his rooms."

"You will be welcomed whenever you wish Mr. Holmes, of course, but I'm afraid the police made a terrible mess of things when they were there."

"There may yet be some illustrative points to be gleaned," he said, "and I would like to get a list of his friends and associates, addresses, and..."

"I have them all here for you," said she, pulling the folded sheet from her little bag.

"A long list," said he, handing it over to me.

"It is divided into friends, business interests, and those attached to his rowing."

"Does he still row?" Holmes asked, surprised.

"From time to time," Mrs. Fyldene answered, "but it is nothing to compare with the hours he devoted to the sport during his college days."

We made plans to join her at her home in the afternoon and when I returned from showing her out, a formality shown only to the special few, I found Holmes at the table bent over the list.

"What a remarkable and beautiful woman," I observed.

"I leave such considerations to you Watson," my friend replied. "What I want to know," said he, sitting up and fixing his eyes upon me, "is what kind of secret could be so great or so terrible that in order to keep it from the world, Mrs. Elizabeth Fyldene, neé Osborne, would risk the life of her own son?"[10]

---

[10] The English adoption of the French term, neé, predated Victorian England, but it was the Victorians who made it all the fashion. The term is used to designate a woman's maiden name and still survives as a holdover in some circles.

Dr. John Watson, MD, Ashburn House, London, 1884

Chapter 2 – The Fog

As our cab made its way through London on our way to Ashburn House I considered Holmes' words regarding Mrs. Henry Fyldene's secret and how such a thing might endanger her son.

The afternoon was the first in several weeks which did not carry the chill reminder that winter was approaching quickly.

"If you gentlemen would wait here," said the footman, showing us into the salon of Ashburn House, the residence of the Fyldene's, "I will inform the mistress of your arrival."

The man stood and watched us for a moment longer, as if he would assure himself that we would in fact stay in the room to which he'd assigned us, then he scurried away with a shuffling gait. Holmes ignored his impertinence and took a leisurely turn about the large, tastefully decorated and comfortably appointed room. He admired several of the family pictures and portraits, even going so far as to pick one or two up and look at them more closely. From what I saw the Fyldene's were a handsome family, although I knew such considerations meant little enough to Holmes' analytical mind.

After this he went and stood before the front window which looked out upon the other fine homes which lined Park Street. I thought I could imagine his very thoughts at that moment, for the scene was nothing like looking down upon Baker Street. After a moment I took a comfortable chair in the corner and leafed through the papers which were stacked just there upon a side table.

We waited while I'd became absorbed in an article relating several new developments in the murder of James Richardson in Leeds in 1882.[11]

---

[11] James Richardson, a glass bottle maker, was last seen with Mary Fitzpatrick. She subsequently pawned his silver watch

"I expect that you are Mr. Henry Fyldene, the Elder," Holmes said, suddenly and apparently without reason. It seemed strange to me as he hadn't turned from the window and I believed he must be talking either to himself or to me, as we were the only ones in the room. When I looked up, however, I found a tall, thin man standing just inside the door of the salon, with one thumb hooked pugnaciously into the side of his vest. He had cold eyes and wore a humorless expression.

Only then did I realize my friend had used that ingenious technique which he had developed and referred to as, "refractory surveillance." Holmes' most famous application of the method had used a highly polished silver coffee pot, but today he'd used a windowpane as his mirror. He'd perfected the method and while he appeared to be looking out the window of Ashburn House, which he also could do, he had actually positioned himself to use the window to see behind him and to the side, upon the doorway.

My friend must have expected the footman to inform the master, and not the mistress of the house, and so he had waited in his position. Only then did he turn and face Mr. Fyldene.

---

and gold chain. Richardson was then discovered dead in the mill pond. Her trial took place in November 1882, as a murder and robbery case at the York Winter Assizes. She was found not guilty of murder, as evidence was lacking, but was found guilty of theft and sentenced to six years penal servitude.

Henry Fyldene

I was struck at once by the similarity of the two men. Physically they mirrored each other, both being tall and lithe. As to their appearances both had piercing blue eyes although, as I had noted, Fyldene's were cold and indifferent or even cruel, where Holmes' were sharp and inquisitive. Each man had a high, broad forehead, with a slightly retreating hair line.

"You may think yourself clever Mr. Holmes," Henry Fyldene remarked, "but to serious minds you only appear as a poser and *an exhibitionist*."

"A genial welcome I see," Holmes replied as he walked up to within inches of the man.

"That's more than I ever planned on saying to you, so now, if you will not remove yourself from my home, I'll beat you from the property myself."

I could have told the man that his scenario was not likely to work out, for Holmes was as gifted a cane-fighter as I'd ever seen enter the ring, but at that moment Mrs. Fyldene appeared upon the spot and shockingly reprimanded her husband.[12]

"Henry," she cried, obviously horrified by his behavior, "these gentlemen are *my guests*."

The man wilted briefly under his wife's sudden and daunting rebuke, for the rule of hospitality was an old and established one in the Kingdom and he had clearly not expected his wife to find him out. Soon enough though he recovered.

"My wife does not enjoy the privilege of asking *questionable men* into my home without my permission," he shot back, without looking at her.

"*Your home*?" she said, flatly and in a manner which clearly informed us that Ashburn House had been purchased with Osborne money.

---

[12] Victorian Cane-Fighting developed into the combat form known as Bartitsu near the end of the 19th Century.

"Do not trouble yourself upon our account Mrs. Fyldene," Holmes said, calmly, "I assure you I've already seen all I needed to."

With that we took our leave and walked out upon Park Street to hail a cab.

"Already seen all you needed to?" I enquired.

"Of course Watson, I would have welcomed the opportunity to have gone through the place with a fine-toothed comb..."

"But?"

"But even in so short a time I gathered even more than I believed would be possible."

"But Holmes, you were only in the salon and even then it was for just a few minutes."

"Thirteen minutes," said he, in that precise way of his, "but it was more than enough to illuminate this...surprising darkness."

"Then what have you to report?" I asked, as Holmes got the attention of a passing cabbie.

"I know how you appreciate a clear and simple line of inquiry Watson," said he, as we took our seats, "but I must say that I'm inclined to make the family portrait, which was among the handsome collection gathered upon the piano, the starting point of my investigation."

"The photograph?" I stuttered. "A photograph indeed, of the Fyldene family, that is the starting point of... surprising darkness, as you put it?"

"We've made excellent progress," he insisted.

I shook my head in wonder and confusion.

"Well I must be very slow for I admit I do not see anything clearly."

"My dear fellow," said he, "you will find that the world is full of obvious things which no one ever notices. It is almost enough to argue that our species has developed a shared myopia over the ages, perhaps as a mechanism for dealing with a superabundance of minutia or detail now present in our world. Mankind now simply blocks out vast chunks of life."

"I fear it is not as simple as you imagine it," I pointed out. "The practice of observation, upon which you have ordered your life, is neither as natural nor as easy for others as you would like to believe. Rather than seeing this as a shortcoming residing with the great herd of humanity, I see it more as the gift of your own unique development. You are, I would suggest, much more the recipient of a rare and beneficial mutation, if you will, than that the mass of humanity suffers under some great and debilitating blindness."

Holmes hung his head and sighed palpably as the cab rocked and swayed upon the cobbles.

"As a species Watson we inevitably feel pity for the blind."

"It is logical to have compassion," I replied.

"Yet my experience has shown me that it is those very people who have sight who are among the most impaired. In fact, they often appear to barely notice what is before their own faces."

"Then, in your view, it is the blind who see?"

"I would propose to you my friend, that many who do not have the benefit of vision exhibit both a remarkable awareness of what is around them as well as heightened ability to sense what others may be feeling."

"There is a compensatory reaction I suppose, among the other senses," I said, in an effort to give my friend's theory a logical explanation.

"I only say it to point out why I question who is truly blind and who is merely *physically so.*"

"So tell me what you saw in thirteen minutes, which I did not?"

"Everything Watson."

"Everything?" I replied, in disbelief. "Then you know where young Henry is?"

"In short I do," said he, well-pleased.

"Then could you not have relieved his parent's fears back there?

"Is that how you saw it Watson? That is how it appeared to you?" he asked, clearly wanting an answer. "I refer to Mr. Henry Fyldene, the Elder, of course. Did he really appear to you to be overcome with worry and concern for his eldest son and namesake?"

"Well no," I replied, surprised even by my own answer.

Holmes words now made me consider what it was I'd really seen in the father, for he certainly didn't strike me as a man fraught with worry.

"He seemed most sedate and calm," I finished.

"And combative as well Watson, you cannot overlook that."

"All this may simply be his manner," I offered.

"You are ever the apologist and the defender my dear fellow. As Goethe said, a man sees in the world what he carries inside himself," said he.[13] "It is one of the things I admire most in you my friend. If only the world contained half the goodness you forever attempt to imbue it with, what a paradise we would then possess. So have I been wrong in my reading of poor Mr. Henry Fyldene, the Elder, and *all of that* was simply his manner while under great tension? Or is it possible that you are wrong in crediting him with noble sentiments which he in no way feels?"

Holmes had cornered me and it had been well done at that. I did tend to see goodness where there sometimes was little or none to be had. I'd gotten that trait from my Grandmother and I had several family members to attest to it. It was also true that I argued for a certain innocence in the actions of others, rather than suspect them of low intentions from the outset.

"I can admit that he did indeed appear in an odd light in view of the loss of his son."

"Oh dear me!" Holmes exclaimed, mockingly. "I must have a look at the man."

---

[13] Johann Wolfgang von Goethe, German polymath, writer, poet, statesman, and scientist. Died in Weimar Germany 1832.

"No doubt you already did," I said.

"Was that what you were doing," I continued, "when you approached him so closely? Such a thing would be just like you, you know."

"You know me so well in just a few years…"

"If it is so then it is the result of hard work," I remarked, "but would you have preferred it if I had stayed as I was and not progressed, even as little as I have?"

"Not for worlds Watson," he declared.

"Then why are you doing this? Is it all to extend the suspense? And will you tell me now or must I wait even longer?"

"You know my love of the dramatic Watson, but I promise even you would find my deductions *hard to believe*."

"After all we've gone through together, what could I possibly be hard to believe now?"

"I'm fairly sure that you would find what I have to say, a good fit for that category."

"I suppose you have a point," I agreed. "When you said that the picture of the Fyldene family was the starting point for your investigation, I found that hard to comprehend."

"Indeed Watson and yet it is my firm belief that it has a direct bearing upon the complex mystery which now swirls all around the disappearance of Henry Fyldene, the Younger."

"And you arrived at this in thirteen minutes?"

"I could have arrived at it in thirteen seconds," said he, confidently. Then noticing my expression he said, "I assure you."

"It seems a very tenuous thing upon which to base your entire investigation."

"Yet it has long been an axiom of mine that the little detail is infinitely the most vital, has it not?"

"Yes I've heard you say something to that effect once or twice before."

"Then I'll proceed by asking what you thought when you entered the salon my fine fellow."

I thought for a moment before I spoke.

"It was tastefully decorated," I remarked, "and comfortably appointed, with an excellent view of Park Street."

"You see Watson, but I am sorry to say you do not observe. Never trust to general impressions but concentrate your mind upon the details."

"The details," I replied, "like the golden paisley upon the piano?"

"Like the family photograph upon the golden paisley, upon the piano," he said, philosophically. "The fool takes in all the lumber he comes across, so that the knowledge which might be useful to him gets crowded out, or at best is jumbled up with a lot of other things, so that he has a difficulty in laying his hands upon the useful when he needs it. The key is always to identify the important details from the dross."

"Alright then," I answered, not a little annoyed by my friend's lecturing, "and what important details did the family photograph reveal to you? And how is it of such significance that it is the starting point for your entire investigation?"

"Ah alas Watson, here we are, home at last."

With that Holmes leaped from the Hansom and was through the door and gone before I'd even reached up to pay the cabbie.

I closed the door behind me and shook my head. In some ways my friend was a bundle of contradictory impulses.

He was impatient for information and could never have the news full enough or fast enough. Conversely he was the stingiest man I'd ever known when it came to sharing the information he'd gleaned.

"You cannot put it off forever," I called out as I reached the landing.

When I entered the sitting room, however, I was surprised to find we were not alone.

"Inspector Redgrave has joined us Watson," Holmes declared, as he bent over a large book.

"Inspector," I said, nodding as I hung my coat and hat and put my gloves and walking stick aside.

Launcelott Redgrave was a quiet man of solid habits and a steady nature, possessing a good mind, disciplined approach, and that firm bulldog jaw which was so common at Scotland Yard. His record in distant York was rumored to be the stuff of greatness. I didn't know about all of that but it was certainly evidence of a workmanlike detective who had risen as high as he could go up there.

"There is nothing right with Mr. Redgrave that Lestrade and Gregson will not soon set at naught," Holmes had predicted early on. As if to prove my friend correct the new detective quickly fell in line behind the others, more like a rookie to the force than a veteran and their equal or superior in skill.

"Dr. Watson," said he, shaking my hand.

"To what do we owe the pleasure of this visit Inspector Redgrave? Or should I take it this is an official call?" Holmes asked, as he motioned the man to the settee and dropped into his own chair beside the fire with a huff.

"I need not explain to you gentlemen that I am very much the new man in London and at the Yard and, taking my wife's advice this once, I didn't come down here in my usual manner."

"Which is to say, a bit rougher?" Holmes noted.

"Which is to say, like the notorious bull-loosed-in-the-fine-china-shop," Redgrave admitted.

Here the man nodded over crossed arms.

"I noticed your *gentle* approach," Holmes said.

"As to that, it was always going to be a passing fancy of mine Mr. Holmes, for it is impossible for me to harness my aggressive nature for very long, even when I set myself to do it."

"So would I be correct in taking this visit as your coming-out, your official introduction to London society as it were? And that from now on we can expect to see less of the debutante and more of the proverbial bull."

"My actual coming out occurred at the Yard an hour or so ago and it made a bit of a splash if what I heard was anything to go on. This here is simply a courtesy call upon you gentlemen. Even though I'll no doubt find it hard going 'round the Yard in the near future, everything I've heard about you two from the lads makes me very much hope that we can work successfully together, hereafter."

"And you believe they understood your point of view then, an hour or so ago, at the Yard?"

"I do Mr. Holmes, as I called Inspector Lestrade a pig-headed fool it would be hard to imagine I'd be misunderstood in my meaning."

"And did you see Gregson?" I asked.

"I believe I referred to him as an arrogant lout," Redgrave said, with a nervous laugh. "It was either that or an upstart knave, I'm afraid that in the heat of the moment I don't recall my precise wording."

"And how will your missus react to this news?" Holmes asked, honestly curious.

"She'll understand," our visitor replied matter-of-factly. "You see we've been married, well, over a decade now. So with all my faults I at least have no more surprises for her. In fact, that was one of my selling points to her, if you follow, for I told her I was an open man and if she'd have me, she'd have me at my worst, as just exactly what she saw, with no little shocks to come out later and upset her plans."

"A patient woman then?" I offered.

"An Angel and a Saint Dr. Watson. A thousand times the woman I dreamed I'd get and ten-thousand times the woman Launcelott Aquinas Redgrave deserved; God knows. Though how I managed to get hold of such a creature I'll never know. And if I still have a job tomorrow I can tell you she'll light a taper candle and give a dozen thank heavens before the day is out."

"You think it would be a miracle then, if you still have your job tomorrow I mean?" I said.

"Indeed Doctor, of that I have no doubt."

"First-class inspectors aren't growing on trees," I said, reassuringly.

"It's kind of you to say so Sir, but from what I've heard about you, well, I shouldn't be surprised."

"And what have you heard?" Holmes enquired.

"Around the Yard they do say that the Doctor is the best you'll find anywhere in the Old Country."

I was surprised to think that I was held in such esteem by the rank and file for neither Holmes nor

I had ever been given much more than a cold reception by the higher-ups.

"But as to your *coming out*," Holmes said, "you didn't agree with Gregson regarding the course of your investigation?"

"I did not Mr. Holmes. It's been weeks and in my opinion he's made a pig's ear of this whole disappearance case. I suppose I could've handled things a bit better though. After all, the big bosses ordered me to shadow their man through the investigation, to get myself familiar with their way of doing things you see, down here in the great metropolis."

"Indeed!" Holmes huffed, as he'd often taken a dim view of *their way* of doing things in the great metropolis.

"So I wondered if you might have some advice for me or if you'd be willing to give a hardworking man a little shove down the right path, as it were."

"Do I take it correctly that Inspector Lestrade is on the Tottenham Court Road Mystery, with the unidentified torso?" Holmes asked, referring to a case which had shared the front pages of the papers with the disappearance of Henry Fyldene for the past month.[14]

"That's right and Gregson has the Fyldene's."

"Interesting," my friend replied, mysteriously.

---

[14] This case known as the Tottenham Court Road Mystery centered upon the discovery of body parts in that area and also in Bedford Square, in October of 1884.

"Why do you ask Mr. Holmes?"

"Ah yes," I thought to myself, "now I'll get some answers," for Holmes had successfully kept me in the dark all the way across town.

"I suppose we might be able to give you a little something Inspector Redgrave," said he, "in the hope of finding a good partner in our fight against the criminal elements."

"I wish to heavens you would, Mr. Holmes, as this might be my only chance to get it right."

"What think you Watson?"

Our visitor was excited by the possibility of a boost up from none other than Mr. Sherlock Holmes himself, and he looked eagerly to me. I was now thirty-two and my stories in the Strand Magazine had made my friend a well-known name in Britain. I found it strange indeed that men like Henry Fyldene, who knew so little of the dark world of criminology, could look down upon my friend for his status as an amateur, while the most seasoned inspectors in the nation entertained nothing but the highest hopes of working with him. Beyond that, virtually every policeman we met upon the streets of every village, town, and city, the length and breadth of the old country, professed an open admiration and respect for Holmes. My friend's scientific method for dealing with crime had not only made him famous, but it also provided me the material to insure the continuation of that fame, amateur or not!

"If Inspector Redgrave would be willing to work *both ways* with us," I said, looking at Holmes, "I think it might prove beneficial."

My point was a simple one. Lestrade, Gregson, and several of the others at Scotland Yard, were always happy to receive Holmes' little insights and revelations, but they rarely provided him with anything useful in return. When they weren't in need of his help they made themselves scarce. There was one exception among them and that was a fellow named Bradford Barton. Having worked only a couple cases with him thus far, however, it was still early days.

"For goodness' sake!" Redgrave exclaimed. "Of course I'd be honored to work hand-in-hand with you gentlemen. Things have to be fair for both sides and not just for the Gregson's and the Lestrade's of the world. I can vouch you won't find me forgetful either gentlemen. It'll all be two-ways with me, you can be sure of it."

We clapped hands all around and formalized our secret alliance right there in our sitting room, then Holmes took up his rosewood pipe and filled it from a Persian slipper.

He never failed to have a foil pouch of his favorite black shag tobacco, Sillem's, shoved down in toe of the slipper he kept on a hook on the wall, just to the right of his chair.[15]

---

[15] Sillem's London Blend™ - Sillem's is one of the oldest names in tobacco. Source: pipedia.org.

After this he gave the Inspector a little nod and handed the slipper over to him. I took out my usual blend, an Arcadia Mixture, and soon bluish rings were rising toward the ceiling.

"So Inspector, you believe the case of the torso murder and the case of the missing Fyldene lad are parallel?"

"Well yes," said he, confused, "aren't they? The two could not possibly be linked...could they?"

My friend's question was clear. Either the two cases were parallel and ran along with no shared connections at all, or they were linked somehow. The odds of the latter option were so low as to be laughable, but I could only shrug, having not yet heard Holmes' insights from Ashburn House.

"Would you believe it if I told you they were linked rather than parallel?"

"I would believe you Mr. Holmes, but I would believe no one else. No offense Doctor."

I nodded in understanding. The idea that the two cases, which all of London had believed were separate, actually shared some commonalities was an incredible leap, even if the man proposing it was Sherlock Holmes.

"Linked," Redgrave muttered, "but how Sir?"

"There's the rub," Holmes admitted, "beyond which I've found that every problem, no matter how complex, becomes almost childishly simple once I've explained it to someone."

With this he gave me a sidelong glance.

"I've often made that very comment to Mr. Holmes," I confessed to Inspector Redgrave.

"And I can't tell you how much I appreciate that there is someone involved in this whole dirty business Mr. Holmes, who can see through the thick fog, even if it isn't me."

Chapter 3 – Granby Street

"This is a twisted business," Holmes agreed, "but may I ask what you were doing in September of '73 and again in June of '74 Inspector?"

"So those were important times were they Mr. Holmes?" the man asked, clearly amused, as he worked to recall those times. "September of '73 saw me a married man and newly promoted."

"An auspicious time for you and the missus then Inspector Redgrave?"

"Indeed it was. I was married and promoted sergeant in the York Constabulary both. I got my stripes the following month. As to June of '74, I was preparing a nursery in our flat, when I wasn't collaring blackguards that is. Our first child was born in early August, she being just ten now."

"And do you have any recollection of what was going on down here…in the Metropolis?"

"I can't say as I do Sir. As hard as it may be to believe, those outside London have lives of their own that sometimes requires all their attention."

"And you Watson?"

"I was in college, but wasn't there some ugly business around then, like this Tottenham Court Road case? In Battersea I believe."

"A good memory," Holmes remarked, putting his pipe to his lips and clapping for me. "The Battersea Mystery they called it and it was never solved. A portion of a woman's trunk was found in Battersea, thus giving the case its name. It was followed in short order by the discovery of another body part at Nine Elms. Then the head was found in Limehouse, an arm somewhere else, and the pelvis in Woolwich. By this time the police could reassemble most of a body. Oddly enough however," Holmes said, as he paused to pull upon his pipe, "the nose and chin had been defaced and the poor woman had been…*scalped*."

"Scalped!" I exclaimed.

"Yes indeed Watson, scalped!"

"But why is that any stranger than the rest it?"

"Well Inspector, although my insights were not considered by Scotland Yard at the time of the earlier crimes, each of these last three atrocities, the nose, chin, and scalping, were punishments common among several of the native tribes of the Indians of North America."[16]

"You mean, with the red Indians?"[17]

"Yes Inspector, although we must agree that scalping itself has a long history which goes far beyond North America."

"Alright, Mr. Holmes, I can admit as much," Mr. Redgrave offered. "But do you really expect me to believe that one of those folk came across and was secretly behind that Battersea business?"

"No Inspector, that would be absurd."

"I'm glad to hear you say it Holmes," I replied, for it had appeared to me as well that my friend was pointing us in that direction. "So what is the significance of the last three mutilations?"

"Is it not obvious?" Holmes asked, earnestly, as he stared at me.

---

[16] Several Plains and Southwestern tribes used some or all of these methods. Some were used in warfare while others were applied as punishments, for infidelity for example.

[17] Red Indians, the archaic term for American Indians, was in use long before Victorian Age, as a way to differentiate them from the "Indians" of India, who were commonly referred to as East Indians.

"Obvious," I repeated, "not to me."

"Nor to me Mr. Holmes," the Inspector said.

"Prior to the war with the American colonists," Holmes began, sounding more like a professor in a stuffy classroom in Oxford than the world's only consulting detective, "a group of men in Boston settled upon a plan."

"The Tea Party," I offered.[18]

"Several of those involved dressed as Natives."

"To throw off the authorities and escape the consequences no doubt," Redgrave replied.

"No Inspector, for no actual tribesmen could possibly have made their way unimpeded to the Boston Docks in 1773 and no one at the time seriously believed that the tribes, who had been pushed farther west, had anything to do with destroying the East India Company's tea."

"Well then, what is your point Mr. Holmes?"

"Just this, that the men involved in that raucous act dressed as Natives simply because the mode and dress of those people was familiar to them. In the same way it is just as obvious that the person who carried out the Battersea murder/mutilation was a student of other cultures."

"I say that really is clever," the Inspector said.

"Sadly that atrocity was repeated nine months later, in June of '74, when another dismembered torso, this time bearing one leg, was found in the

---

[18] The Boston Tea Party, December 16th, 1773.

Thames at Putney. Those crimes were judged 'Willful murder by person or persons unknown.'"

"And now we have a repeat of these ghastly crimes," the Inspector observed. "An imitator Mr. Holmes, or the first fiend returned like a ghost from the blooming past?"

"That is a novel way of saying it Inspector."

"How is that Sir?"

"To say that the fiend had returned from the past, that was *illustrative*."

I was used to my friend's ways by now, but poor Inspector Redgrave was lost to Holmes' point.

"I wonder Watson, if you have one of the early articles on this Tottenham Court case somewhere there in one of your several stacks?"

"I do," I said, pulling a copy of the Pall Mall Gazette from the pile of papers I kept for their clippings. In imitation of my friend I'd started keeping my own reference journals.

"Would you read it out for us, just as a review of the facts as we know them."

"The Discovery of Human Remains," I said, reading the title of the article. "Acting under the personal direction of Inspector Langrish, Chief the Detective Department at Bow-Street, the police are engaged in making the strictest inquiries with reference to the discovery of human remains at King's Cross Station, Bedford Square, and Fitzroy Square. The circumstances under which various body parts were found have been made public, but up to the present the affair is surrounded in mystery."

"It will be remembered," I continued reading, "that almost simultaneously with the discovery of a thigh and some human flesh in Bedford Square, it was reported that a skull and another portion of the body were found at King's Cross Station. Further remains were found in the area of Fitzroy Square. The evidence was given to Dr. Samuel Lloyd for examination, and at first he believed that it was possible that the different portions might belong to separate bodies. Closer examination, however, has convinced the doctor that all belong to the body of one young woman. In each case the remains were covered with the same kind of disinfectant. It is conclusively proved that death must have taken place between four and six months since. Additionally, upon the arm found in Bedford Square there is a tattoo mark about two inches above the wrist apparently representing half of a bracelet, the marks being by a bright red ink color. This has led to the supposition that the victim was a prostitute."

"I remember reading that grisly piece myself a while back," the Inspector noted. "I must say that it does not improve upon familiarity nor does it bear repeating."

"All the same gentlemen, the solution is there."

Holmes' clear statement and its unbelievable implications stunned us.

Henry Fyldene

"The solution *is there*" Redgrave exclaimed, "in the article?"

"Yes and so I would recommend that you read it again, only this time with your minds prepared to glean the vital information from the dross."

"You are serious Holmes?" I enquired.

"Of course Watson," said he, staring into the fire without another word.

"Would you read it again Doctor?"

I went slowly through it a second time, looking up occasionally to mark points with the Inspector which I thought might possibly prove significant. When I finished Holmes asked us for our thoughts.

"Now that you know beyond a doubt, that the solution of the infamous Torso Murders resides in that clipping," said he, "what great revelations do you have for me?"

Inspector Redgrave looked at me and shrugged and I, knowing my friend's high expectations, knew that I had to do my best.

"The killer faces certain difficulties," I offered, nebulously.

"Of course," Holmes replied, "but specifically?"

"Well, who can go about the city with a torso and not be noticed, even during the hours of darkness? Or a torso with a leg still attached? And the article said the woman had been dead for between four to six months. Even disinfected, I mean, *it is different* from preserved and that in itself would present its own *peculiar* smell."

"Oh well done Watson. Indeed, well done," Holmes said, seriously. "So then how did the killer do it gentlemen, for it was most certainly done?"

"I have two ideas upon that point," I replied, happy that I'd done well thus far.

"And I am eager to hear them," Holmes replied.

"First then," I ventured, "he would require an accomplice and a private carriage as he could not conduct such a business from a cab, could he? I cannot imagine going about town with a human torso, and even if the cabby had no idea what his passenger was doing, he would certainly realize later when the item appeared in the press, that he had delivered a man about town with odd parcels and to all those same places. And the police have had no such witnesses come forward."

"This really is most refreshing my dear fellow," Holmes remarked, nodding as he sometimes did when he was well-pleased. "Now for your second idea, if you would be so good."

"That if he has no accomplice and must see to the whole thing himself, he'd require a cart, and one which would not appear conspicuously at such odd hours. It would be more challenging as he must leave the cart unattended for periods as he carried out his macabre march about the metropolis, but I think *it might* be possible. The only thing I would add," said I, growing more confident, "is that the man must be quite odd and fit within a very narrow set of requirements."

"How so Doctor?" Inspector Redgrave asked.

"For one he could not own a carriage or even a cart without capital. Then there is the location of his mutilations. If he is a family man how could he risk conducting such a villainy in his own home?"

"True," the Inspector said.

"And as the corpse remained for months, that would spell trouble for the man," Holmes offered.

"So he must own or hold a lease upon a place, and not just any place either," said I.

"Both of which would require additional access to capital," Holmes added, now very excited.

"Yes," said I, "for the place must be such that it answers your theorem Holmes."

"Which theorem is that?" the Inspector asked.

"It is more accurately a principle," Holmes said, philosophically, "that the vilest alleys in London do not present as black a record of crime as does our glorious countryside."

"That is a *dark* observation," Redgrave offered, "but I suppose there could be some truth in it."

"So," I continued, "this fiend's workplace must be either remote enough to shield his activities, or in among such a noisome collection of neighbors in the city as to not draw *unwanted attention*."

Holmes stared upon me as if I were a Malayan Orangutan which had just walked in and sat down.

He had often observed that, while I was not myself luminous, I was a good conductor of light.

"Watson," said he, finally, "you have excelled yourself and if you continue on in this vein I will confess that I have underrated you."

"Then I've struck the head of the nail full," I said, with some self-importance. It was a double pleasure to shine before the Inspector as well. The feeling was indeed new to me and I liked it.

"I am delighted to say, my good fellow, that most of your insights are surely...of value. If they are not precisely accurate in every point, they surely are in the main. The man is certainly a gentleman or at least a man of easy capital, for the reasons you pointed out and several more as well. A working man dependent upon a job for his livelihood could never carry out all the various actions required for the crime. If he maintains a job he must also possess adequate funds to carry out the crime simultaneously. I prefer your idea that he works alone as well, for an accomplice in such a grim business, even if one could be had, would simply be too great a risk. I believe we will find his workplace, as you put it, in the city where he can gain access with a short journey from his home. It will be among unsavory neighbors, as you said, perhaps as a tannery or slaughterhouse, or some such place, where the smells, sounds, and all the goings-on would provide an adequate cover for his business."

"So he has a cart or wagon?" I asked.

"A coal cart would be among the most simple and innocuous and would present no great cost for a man of moderate capital, although it would be prohibitive for most of the city's inhabitants. Such vehicles are ubiquitous in the early hours and he need not even own the horses."

"No," the Inspector offered, "he could schedule them and a pair could be had by the day for a pittance compared with only them."

"And a hidden cavity under a light covering of coal could be easily built and accessed," I added.

Holmes nodded with satisfaction.

"Then I was right? I found the solution."

"As to that Watson I'm afraid you've missed the mark completely, but you must not allow that to deter you, for you've done well."

"Missed it?" I stuttered, for I believed I'd gotten a great deal from the article."

"To the extent your deductions went, however, you provided the Inspector and the Yard with a great deal to go on."

"But that was all?"

"No my dear Watson, not all, but you did not touch upon the one *unique clue* which narrows a multitude of criminals to just one fiend."

"I must say though," the Inspector insisted, "that I have never seen such a demonstration of pure detection before in my life as Dr. Watson just put on here Mr. Holmes."

Mr. Launcelott Redgrave's words of sincere praise were not lost upon me and for a moment I thought that I must feel a little of what my friend, Holmes, had felt so often and upon a regular basis.

"You see Watson? You've done well and you now have the good Inspector's opinion to join together with mine, should you have any doubts upon the subject."

"But I was pursuing *the solution* you spoke of!"

"In that case I would suggest that we look now at the clue of the tattoo mark," said he.

"The tattoo?" I repeated.

"It was about two inches above the wrist," the Inspector reminded, "and in the general form of a bracelet in red ink so they said."

"But you have not seen the tattoo Inspector?" Holmes asked.

"I was engaged with Gregson upon this Fyldene trouble and he didn't go in for boosting Lestrade."

"It was the tattoo that led them to the notion that the victim was a prostitute," I said.

"Yes, yes, for no decent woman would have any such marks upon her person, however, this is the crux of the case gentlemen. It is upon this point that everything turns."

"Though you say it's so Sir, you've lost me."

"If the appearance of a little tattoo upon the wrist is enough in our society, to turn the doctor and the police toward the conclusion that the body they have before them is that of a prostitute, then we must ask ourselves if we might not be standing a bit too close to the compass?"

"What are you saying Mr. Holmes?"

"Mr. Holmes refers to the disturbance which may be done to a magnetic compass," I answered. "Which may be disturbed by so little a thing as a man's belt buckle, pocket watch, guard chain, or his fobs being in too close a proximity to it."

"And from a false reading upon the compass a great error may easily follow."

"Then are you implying that this dead woman *isn't* a prostitute at all Mr. Holmes?"

"Do you recall Scrooge's response to the ghosts who visited him in the night?" Holmes answered the Inspector's question with a question.[19]

"That they might be caused by an undigested bit of beef...or a piece of underdone potato, is that what you are referring too?" the Inspector said.

"Yes," I said, quoting what I recalled, "there's more of gravy than of grave about you!"

"The critical thing to understand Inspector, is that it is a capital mistake to theorize *before* you have all the evidence! It cannot fail to distort the judgment to the detriment of truth. You would do well to memorize the point Sir," Holmes stressed.

"Then by assuming they know who this woman is, what they've really done is misjudge her."

"Not only that Inspector Redgrave, but they've also missed the key to her true identity, though it is right there staring them in the face!"

"So while the police comb through the docks, Southwark, Whitechapel, and the like, the usual places for a missing prostitute, the victim had nothing to do with those areas."

"You are beginning to arrive Inspector. They've taken the wrong lead but let me show you this."

With this Holmes pulled a slip of paper from his pocketbook and handed it across with his old magnifying lens.

---

[19] A Christmas Carol, by Chas. Dickens, Published by Chapman & Hall, London, ©1843.

Inspector Redgrave examined it first and then handed both the lens and paper over to me without a word.

"The red rose of Lancaster?" I muttered when I saw the sketch drawn upon the paper in pencil.

"Is that an image of the tattoo Mr. Holmes?"

"Indeed it is, but it has no more to do with Lancaster than it had to do with a prostitute for that matter."

Now my friend pulled one of his large reference volumes up from beside his chair.

"Compare the illustration here with the sketch I drew from the poor woman's wrist Watson."

I opened to the bookmark and saw the same simple, five-petaled flower in Holmes' book.

"The arms of the House of *Rosenberg*," I read.

"The House of Rosenberg?" Inspector Redgrave repeated. "Rosenberg? I've never heard of it."

"Read on Watson, there is little enough left."

"As seen at Hohenfurth Abbey, Bohemia."

"Bohemia, what is this all about Mr. Holmes?"

"Now compare the sketch with this," my friend said, ignoring the Inspector for the moment and turning to another page.

"The Red Rose of Lancaster, the heraldic badge of the Royal House of Lancaster."

"You can see that the Lancaster Rose is a bi-petaled flower with the smaller atop the larger," Holmes explained. "Notice that the larger flower has the tip of its top petal pointing directly at 12 o'clock. Meanwhile, the Rosenberg Rose has only one set of petals with the tip of the bottom petal pointing at 6 o'clock."

"And it's this Rosenberg Rose that matches your drawing Mr. Holmes, almost exactly."

"Accounting for my artistic limitations, the two are identical Inspector," Holmes agreed.

"Then she was never a prostitute?" I said.

"It is far more likely that she came here as an immigrant from Bohemia," said he.

"Consider also," Holmes continued, "that a woman making their living upon the streets, as they supposed this victim did, would very naturally be known to a multitude of people."

"If our killer had targeted one of those women then they would have been missed," I observed.

"You may be right," Redgrave said.

"The probability certainly lies in that direction," Holmes said, supporting my notion. "If we take it as a working hypothesis then we have a fresh basis for the identification of this unknown victim and with her come a multitude of other clues."

"Well then, supposing that she was one of the Rosenberg's...from the continent," I said, "what further inferences may we draw?"

"Do none suggest themselves? You know my methods and have done well applying them thus far. Simply apply them again my good fellow."

"Then the murderer waits at the ports for his next victim and being young and inexperienced, the immigrant girl falls prey to him," I theorized.

"What the Doctor says is a real possibility Mr. Holmes. That the man has practiced this method before can be seen by the murders you pointed out in '73 and '74, and no one would miss them."

"I think that we might venture even a little farther than this," Holmes said. "Look at it in this light gentlemen. There have been at least thirteen wars, uprisings, revolts, or insurrections, call them by what you will, in that region of Europe alone and in just the last two generations. This has created a world of chaos and upheaval there and the economies of several countries are bust or in sharp decline. So upon what occasion would a young immigrant woman coming to this country for work be most likely to accept the approach of a stranger waiting at the dock in England?"

Inspector Redgrave dropped his head suddenly into his hands and seemed overcome. He had clearly realized what my friend alluded to.

"You cannot mean it Mr. Holmes, surely?" said he, mysteriously.

"Such an idea disturbs you Inspector?"

"What idea?" I demanded.

"Mr. Holmes is proposing that this devil, this killer, is the very man communicating with these women before they ever reach Britain."

"So they...*expect* to find him waiting?" I asked.

"They walk into his trap and go unwittingly to their death," Holmes said, "and another thing."

"What is that?" I asked, unsure that I wanted to know, for the more my friend described the more my skin crawled at this case.

"In regions of eastern Europe the presence of a discreet and tasteful tattoo, often reflecting the crest or symbol of their great houses, is de rigueur among the finest women."

This information gave us pause.

"This is among the most grotesque cases I've ever known," Inspector Redgrave said, shaken.

This revelation was jolting, even to me and I'd seen a great many monstrous things already. I looked to my friend and Holmes nodded sadly.

"When would these women be most likely to give this man their trust, but upon reaching our shores and finding their future employer awaiting them with a warm welcome, perhaps even with flowers. He wouldn't have to win their confidence as he was the one who'd arranged for them to come. He'd simply provide them the name they expected and they'd follow him. Is it stretching our hypothesis too far then, to propose that this method was used before, as the Inspector has already realized, in '73 and '74? Further, there would be absolutely no one here to miss them."

"So it's the same man," Redgrave muttered.

"He doubtlessly used an alias," Holmes added, "and a mail drop, so any investigation from family, even without the obvious delay of weeks or months, would be doomed from the outset."

"It is diabolical," I agreed.

"The police would have nowhere to start."

"Ah what is this then?" Holmes exclaimed, as our bell was pulled hard.

Billy came in a moment later with a slip of crumpled paper upon the little silver platter.

"The boy?" Holmes asked, taking up the paper.

"Outside Sir, Mrs. Hudson said he was too dirty to walk upon her floors. He has been here before Mr. Holmes and is in terrible fear of...her."

Holmes nodded and placed a gold sovereign on the platter and Billy retreated, closing the door quietly behind him.

"What is this all about Mr. Holmes."

"This?" said Holmes, holding up the paper, "this slip holds the address where you'll find this devil, Inspector Redgrave."

"It's an odd time for such jokes Sir," the man said, indignantly.

"I assure you Inspector that I do not jest. My people have tracked the fiend to his workplace and, as you have asked us for a, how did you put it? *A little shove down the right path wasn't it? Well, here is your little shove. You* can see for yourself, here is your push Inspector Redgrave," Holmes said, handing the slip over, "and it is in just the sort of place we predicted."

Holmes' *people*, as he referred to them, were a pack of street urchins he'd recruited and loosely organized into a unit known as the Baker Street Irregulars. While they weren't much to look at and were often the recipients of upbraiding from Mrs. Hudson's and her housemaid, Mrs. Turner, they were undeniably effective at what they did.

"Thirty-Three Granby Street" Redgrave cried, "and would you believe it, right next to the local coal depot as I recall, but is this trustworthy or might it be...?"

"Unquestionably trustworthy and if you move quickly Inspector, you shall have your man."

"How was that for a shove?" I asked, smiling.

Scotland Yard's newest inspector stood and looked down upon Holmes as if he were beholding Nostradamus himself.

"I never expected such help when I came here Mr. Holmes, but you shall find me grateful Sir. You have the word of Launcelott Redgrave upon that.

"Just one thing before you go Inspector," my friend replied, "for I require a very particular kind of payment for this information."

"Anything Mr. Holmes! The good Lord knows I owe you gentlemen mightily."

"My name must not be connected in any way."

"But then all the credit falls on me?"

"That is the cost of my help."

"It doesn't sound very square if you ask me, but who am I to argue with a man who can identify a mad killer in a city of a million souls and all from comfort of his sitting room and with just the sketch of a tattoo to go on."

Chapter 4 – Mrs. Fyldene's Secret

After Inspector Redgrave had taken his leave to pursue the killer of multiple immigrant women over the span of a decade or more, I took the opportunity to have my questions answered.

"Who is it then? The fiend Redgrave chases."

"I told you Watson, that you'd find it hard to believe," said he.

"But you said those words in reference to the Fyldene Mystery after our visit to Ashburn House, not to the Tottenham Court Road business or the Battersea business."

"You've forgotten what I said about the cases."

"I must have, for I'm unsure what you're talking about now."

"I said the cases were *linked* Watson, *linked!*"

"Yes, linked," I repeated, but the word didn't convey anything to my mind, at least not at first.

"*Linked*," he said again.

"How is such a thing even possible?" Then I understood. "It's him? Henry Fyldene, the Elder, he's the killer of the immigrant women? That's the how the cases are linked," I cried, realizing the man I'd seen at Ashburn House was the killer.

"Who is more vulnerable than the immigrant woman who arrives here young, alone, knowing nothing and no one Watson? And who better to prey upon them than a man who has traveled the world, studied a dozen different cultures, speaks all the diplomatic languages, and possesses both the time and the capital to see to requirements of these crimes?"

"The very thought is...repugnant," I replied.

"Of course it is my good fellow, but did you not realize that the man fit every one of the points you proposed earlier. You were brilliant Watson."

This compliment was almost lost upon me as I struggled to comprehend all that had presented itself to my mind in so short a time.

"But was he even here in '73 and '74?"

"He was," said he, withdrawing a telegram from his pocket and showing me.

"When did you do that?" I enquired, for I had been with him all day.

"Billy sent it off for me this morning, before we left for Ashburn House."

"Then you suspected the man even then?"

"No I can't say that I did, but as he was one of the rare men who fit all the necessary aspects of the Torso Killer, and was thrust so suddenly up before me, as it were, I hoped the telegram would remove him from my suspicions."

"But it did the opposite," I remarked, taking the telegram and reading it.

"Mr. Henry Fyldene took leave to set his affairs in order after the death of his father in Leeds in early 1873. He arrived in England in May of 1873 and returned to Arabia late in 1874."

"So you see my dear friend, everything pointed to the possibility. Then I recognized one of the Irregulars rummaging along Park Street."

Holmes had told me that the most affluent districts were sometimes the most generous with his Irregulars, if the boy was young and traveled alone.

"That's what you were doing in the window," I cried, "that confusing code you developed with all the hand signals."

"The code is simplicity itself," said he, "once you get past the complexities."

"You do realize what you're saying," I replied, "don't you?"

"The boy followed Fyldene after we departed, then sent the message which Inspector Redgrave took away with him."

"Thus the gold sovereign."

"It is my scale of payment after all."

The Irregulars were paid upon a scale which set various rates based upon such imponderables as the *value* of their information, the speed with which they operated and, of course, how well the boys stayed out of trouble. That Holmes' harbored the ulterior motive of helping reform the boys through his employment had been something that had escaped me for the longest time. The power of a gold sovereign, however, was undeniable.

I was not surprised to witness a gradual but steady improvement in both the behavior and appearance of his little troop over the course of the last several years now.

"And what will Redgrave find at Thirty-Three Granby Street?" I asked.

"*A house of horrors* my dear Watson, beyond all imaging." said he, deeply moved. "A veritable nightmare of death like Poe's Pit & Pendulum.[20] No doubt it will be filled with a proliferation of barbaric mementos, personal keepsakes, glass jars, medical equipment, and everything which might appeal to a sick and unbalanced mind."

"You seem very certain when there was really so little to go on," I observed.

"No doubt it seems that way," said he.

"There is more isn't there? You aren't telling me something."

---

[20] The Pit and the Pendulum, by Edgar Allan Poe, Published by Carey & Hart, ©1842.

"Oh Watson! How long have we been together for you have come to know me so well?"

"Four years," I replied.

"Four years hmmm. You must admit it doesn't feel like four years."

"Perhaps not in some ways, but there've been a great many dead bodies, you must admit that."

"No doubt but I would've said a year, eighteen months perhaps, at most, but not four years."

"Well it is," said I.

"I'll wager that Lestrade and Gregson provided long odds on you surviving with me."

"You think they were keeping a book on me then, at Scotland Yard, taking bets, and holding the money?"[21]

"Indubitably Watson and the only thing they wonder at now is how you've kept your sanity all this time."

Holmes was only half in jest, for few in the official services could understand the logic which underpinned his methods. His puzzling manner, unconventional ways, and mercurial nature had done the rest. So there was an element of truth in his speculations.

"As entertaining as the thought is, you still have not answered my question."

---

[21] "A Book" may refer to an individual "Bookie" or a business operating bets. Sometimes referred to as a "sportsbook," it records names of the bettors, odds given, and amounts wagered and "paid out."

"I haven't have I," said he. "But I can tell you that after circling around the salon at Ashburn House, taking everything in, and signaling to my confederate upon the street, when Mr. Fyldene appeared in the doorway I approached him very closely indeed."

"You did," I recalled, "and I took it you were quite offended by the man's words."

"And so I intended it to seem Watson, but in truth I only wanted the excuse to examine the man minutely, from close range."

"You discovered something!" I exclaimed. "I knew it. I figured there was something about the fellow that troubled you, but being all but invisible to me it appeared a mystery."

"One of your subscriptions is for the Lancet," said he, continuing.

My friend's statement was the kind which had seemed like a tangent to me in our first years, but which I now realized was the necessary preamble to explain his answer in depth.

"It is my weekly medical journal and keeps me abreast of the latest advancements. I admit I am much dependent upon it."

"Well Watson, as it happens I'd already read all the available evidence from the last edition of your cherished Lancet before we journeyed to Ashburn House. That information allowed me to examine the man most thoroughly for any related evidence."

"I didn't realize that."

"And did you know, for instance, and quite contrary to the popular opinion, that the victim in the Tottenham Court Road Murder had not been hacked upon at all? Instead, the Lancet reported that it had been most dexterously cut up and neatly disarticulated at the joints. It was only at two points, the hip-joint and shoulder, where a fine-toothed medical-grade saw was used."

"I didn't know," I admitted, "but I hadn't gotten around to the latest edition yet, with all our focus upon the papers."

"Quite understandable," said he, graciously. "I trust that you are, however, more than familiar with the nature and characteristics of proteins Watson, such as makes up human flesh."

"I should say so," I replied.

"Proteins possess an incredible ability to cling to whatever they touch."

"True but what has that to do with Fyldene?"

"I noted no less than six bits of the most minute fragments of bone and flesh upon the outside right shoulder of his suit jacket, all but invisible to the human eye and quite invisible to the wearer himself, due to its location."

"Invisible…yet you saw it."

"I was expecting it or I should say, if Fyldene was our killer I expected that he would not be free of some such clue."

"And his study of other cultures?"

"In the locked cabinet in the salon were two volumes upon the North American Indian by Mr. George Catlin and one on human anatomy. This seemed more than adequate to confirm at least an interest in the subjects."

"But the volumes might easily have been the property of Mrs. Fyldene or even one of the sons."

"True, very true my good fellow, but the note extending from one volume was in a man's hand."

"Again, it could have been the son's," I insisted.

"It was not the hand of a young man," said he, "and the few visible words referred clearly to the removal of an unfortunate woman's nose for the crime of...*infidelity*."

It was only then that I realized that my friend, Sherlock Holmes, was truly the most perfect reasoning and observing machine the world was ever likely to see.

"I must say Holmes, that you proceed from strength to strength."

I could have said much more for the man was, despite his humanity, his eccentricities, and the gaping holes in his knowledge, a genuine dynamo. His ability to see through the most mystifying puzzles and even predict what he might find made him, in many ways, the Nostradamus which the Inspector believed him to be.

"It seems you've cleared up several unsolved cases, considering '73 and '74 as well, all while setting out to solve another case altogether," I observed.

"The linked nature of the crimes made that inevitable Watson," said he, with no reference to my words of praise.

"So where is Henry Fyldene the Younger and what was that question you asked me?"

"You speak of Elizabeth Fyldene's secret."

"Yes, you asked what secret could be so terrible that a mother would risk her son's life rather than reveal it. Did Ashburn hold the answer?"

"It did Watson!"

"It did?" I cried, both pleased and amazed.

"Indeed it did. You remember that I told Mrs. Fyldene I'd already seen all I needed to."

"So you know her secret now and was it such a terrible thing after all?"

"What did you make of the family portrait?" said he, sidestepping my question.

"The one upon the golden paisley cloth, upon the piano, that one?"

"Just so, that one."

"A handsome family," I replied.

"Was there no clue there Watson?"

I must've looked surprised for Holmes laughed.

"It was a fine portrait to be sure," said I, "but of no significance beyond that surely. At least not in helping us find the missing man. How could it?"

"No?" said Holmes, still questioning. "Then let me ask you again why a father would not seem concerned by the disappearance of his son, his eldest son and his namesake at that?"

"There is no reason I can think of. The man must be beside himself with fear and worry."

"But he didn't appear so when you saw him. You said as much."

"Your absolutely right Holmes. It seemed that he was only bothered by your presence."

"Puzzling, isn't it?"

"Indeed now that you mention it."

"Wouldn't a loving father gladly accept help from anyone who might regain him his son?"

"Yes, of course. No matter who it was."

"But Henry Fyldene, the Elder, did not and why he did not is *the question* my good fellow."

"He even threatened violence to be rid of you and you the most proven detective ever known. It is incomprehensible," I insisted.

"And precisely because it is incomprehensible Watson, it is of vital importance."

"And it all comes down to that family portrait you say?"

"No doubt. I only mention it because I have made a particular study of the head and face, as you know. I've identified nine inheritable points."

"I read your monograph," I reminded him, "and you said there were even more points, but you'd narrowed them to the nine most suggestive."

"I based my ideas on a foundation of Mendel's Principles of Heredity."[22]

"Oh," I said, "I see. When you looked at the family portrait of the Fyldene's, you applied your facial identification system to it."

"That's correct Watson and what is more, doing so provided me with vital information."

---

[22] Gregor Mendel's experiments were publicized in 1865, becoming known as "Mendelian Inheritance" they formed the foundation of modern genetics.

I puzzled over my friend's words but could make neither heads nor tails of them.

"The portrait explains why the elder Fyldene is not at all concerned with the recovery of the younger Henry."

I stared in sudden comprehension.

"Are you saying," I stuttered, "can you really be saying that the young man is not Fyldene's son at all Holmes, not even a Fyldene in point of fact?"

My friend smiled.

"Then that would...be *Mrs. Fyldene's secret*."

"I asked you what secret could be so terrible my good fellow. Now you know."

"That woman," I sympathized, "has worked to keep her secret all these years."

"Has she Watson?"

"Well yes, otherwise she would certainly have told us, as it could have had something to do with the case."

"If her husband has so little concern for the boy, how effective do you really think she has been in keeping her secret?"

"And you recognized all of this the instant you saw the picture."

"It was a simple exercise," he said, proudly. "As each parent provides an equal part toward the development of the child, the union of people from the same general ancestral group should produce little variance in the children. After all, each sibling has the same genetic blueprint."

"Although one may have blue eyes and another brown?" I forwarded, neither being a specialist in the field or even Holmes' equal upon the subject.

"That is in the dominant and recessive nature of a gene my good fellow, but the gene given to the children remains the same for all of the offspring. Otherwise it could be said that every sibling has a different genetic makeup, when we know very well that such an eventuality is an utter impossibility."

"So the Fyldene brothers, if they were in fact full brothers, would have been given the same genes by each parent."

"Just so and despite some variance, such as eye and hair color, they would share in several of the same inherited characteristics."

"Yet even I noticed that the sons in the portrait showed a far more marked difference than any similarity," I said, "although I merely glanced at the photograph."

"Yes and the presence of so many photographs from across the years provided a wealth of data upon which to base my deductions. The younger son, who was shown in the front of the portrait, is clearly the result of the melding of both parents. Of this there can be no doubt or question. In fact four of the nine points matched the mother and five matched the father. Mathematically speaking you couldn't escape so obvious a conclusion. As you said, even a glance at the portrait was enough to immediately emphasize the differences."

"I can see now that the younger Henry didn't look at all like the elder Henry," I remarked.

"He shares no points of commonality at all with the supposed father, a virtual impossibility in the real-world Watson. He also has only three points of commonality with the mother. That argues that his real father is not only darker but carries a preponderance of dominant traits. Young Henry has little in common with his brother either, whom we now know to be only his half-brother. Even when they were little children Henry was distinctly darker than his younger brother, who was extremely light, blonde haired, and green-eyed."

"While the older brother has black hair, brown eyes, and olive skin."

"Time Watson, that merciless and unyielding master, revealed what the good lady refused to, and what she had worked so hard to keep secret all these years."

"So her husband didn't realize anything in the beginning," I said.

"Thus the given name of Henry Fyldene, the Younger. The passage of years and the growth and development of the young man, however, made the discovery of the truth inevitable. It became all too obvious to any but Mrs. Fyldene. The exact point at which the father realized his wife's duplicity and the truth about the boy, we cannot say, but we can identify it generally."

"So he did realize it...in time."

"Of that we can be certain Watson and when he did there could be no doubt in his mind about it. He had gone along for years assuming what any husband and father naturally would, that the boy was his. He overlooked the little oddities *at first*."

"It is easily enough done," I admitted. "I had an aunt who was darker than the rest of the family but my grandfather recalled that his grandmother too, had shared that trait."

"Yes and so it goes. Having once accepted it, he considered the variances in his own line, or that of his wife's, and recalled a relative who shared this characteristic or that. Once he'd set aside his doubts it was easier to continue doing so. In time, however, as the boy developed, the differences became more glaring and harder to ignore or reason away. When the Elder finally realized, he may even have been able to deduce the identity of the true father. He would have gone back in time to recall the men who were in his wife's circle at the time of the son's conception."

"Then this explains everything."

"It explains a great deal," Holmes agreed, "but it doesn't necessarily explain where the young man is now or even if he is still alive. It does, however, clarify why the father wished to run me out of his home so swiftly."

"He feared you'd see something, just as you in fact did Holmes!" I exclaimed. "You realize you do have a reputation you know."

"I'm inclined to agree," said he, "and hopefully Inspector Redgrave will run him to ground at last, for such devils have no right to roam the world unfettered."

"No doubt Lestrade will be bothered by being displaced, for he knew nothing of the matter."

"He is one of those who can imagine every victim a prostitute," Holmes huffed, "and all that is required is that she be...a woman."

"There are a good many these days who are notoriously down upon women," I admitted.

"One would think none of them had mothers."

J. B. Varney

Chapter 5 – The House of Blood & Death

"Well, well, what do you make of this?"

It was Inspector Lestrade, who stood just inside the front door of 33 Granby Street, out of the cold.

"That blasted constable, he'll be letting all the riffraff in next," he continued, "mark my word."

"Hello Lestrade," Holmes replied, without any show of having heard the inspector's insult.

"If it isn't Mr. Sherlock Holmes and Dr. Watson, of course, and how did you find out about this grisly corner of the Kingdom?"

Holmes didn't answer and, as such, I followed his lead and said nothing of the short message Inspector Redgrave sent us earlier in the evening, when he discovered that the address Holmes had given him was indeed all that had been expected, and much more.

"Come quickly gentlemen," it read, "for you are sorely needed."

"Another feather in your cap Lestrade or what do we have here?"

"Not in my cap Mr. Holmes!" the man snapped, coldly. "This is all in Inspector Redgrave's show now, though how he came about things still seems a little *unclear* I must say."

"The new man from York?" Holmes said, taking his play even further and feigning ignorance.

"That's right Mr. Holmes, the new man. You'll find him further in but mind you it's dark, and I'm not just speaking about the shortage of light in there either."

Lestrade was clearly put out by the loss of glory he had expected to gain for himself from the case and had nothing more to say as we passed on down the musty hall.

The old building had a solid look to it which, even in the dim hours of late evening, struck me as extremely odd for the neighborhood.

"Fine oak panels on Granby Street?" I noted.

"This area was not always the heart of poverty and despair you see today," Holmes replied. "Even here there was a time when some still had hopes and expectations. The place likely predates the coal dump next door by a good fifty years."

"So what was it?"

"I would have thought you the ideal man to deduce that," said he, tapping the tip of his cane against a small, dust-covered sign barely visible above a side-door.

"Surgery?" I stammered. "A doctor's office?"

"With a modest waiting room up front near Lestrade and, likely, a more substantial private residence above, but such a place couldn't pay its bills here today and not for a long time past."

"It isn't that the poor don't require medical care," I offered, "but even among a great mass of them they couldn't afford to maintain even a modest practice such as this once was."

"Not like Harley Street?" Holmes countered, referring to one of London's most lucrative streets for doctors, surgeons, and specialists.

"No, nothing like Harley Street."

"Then too," he continued, "there is the crime around here to be considered. It would be a rash and reckless doctor indeed to move a wife and children in here today."

There was a tragic truth to Holmes observation.

We walked into what seemed a vast chamber in the dark, lit as it was by only three lanterns, and shadowy forms moved in and out of the golden circles illuminated around each light.

"Over here gentlemen," came the familiar call of Inspector Redgrave.

"We found this house of blood and death when we came storming in here Mr. Holmes."

The Inspector's face was drawn and pale and when he cast the lamp light upon the gray form of yet another dead woman lying upon an old-style examination table, I understood why.

"T'is is an unholy place this," one of the men said, under his breath. Meanwhile, Holmes began as thorough an examination as he could under the circumstances.

"There are no clues there," Redgrave said, "but we all gave it our best try nonetheless."

"Yes," Holmes nodded. Then he proceeded to shock all those gathered around. "She is twenty years old, of a prosperous family, a prolific writer, sadly with poor vision, unable to engage in much physical activity, and was likely hired to serve as a private secretary, but beyond that Inspector, you are quite correct, there are no clues."

The younger policemen who'd only ever heard of Mr. Sherlock Holmes were struck speechless. The Sergeant, Sturken by name, who'd seen my friend in action before, smiled proudly. He'd no doubt told the younger men stories of Holmes.

Redgrave, who'd seen what Holmes could do in the comfort of our sitting room, was awestruck.

"How the devil did you figure all that Sir," said he, after a reverent moment of silence.

"It's magic!" someone said.

I could relate with the man, for I too had been overcome by my friend's extraordinary abilities upon more than on occasion.

"Elementary and quite obvious gentlemen, I assure you," Holmes declared.

"You'll have to forgive me Mr. Holmes but I'll be siding with the constable and calling it magic until you explain yourself."

Holmes looked around the little circle of light and saw a half-dozen expectant faces staring back.

"Well then," said he, "her age was clear from the appearance of the third molars, which usually arrive between the ages of eighteen and twenty-one or twenty-two.[23] The wear upon the teeth justified the older estimate. As to the family's prosperity the deduction was even easier, for you will never find such excellent dental work and in gold at that, except in such a family."

"But how'd ye you know she were a writer?"

The timid voice had come from one of the younger men in the shadows.

"You will note here," my friend said, pointing to a bump upon the side of the middle finger of the right hand which faced the index finger, "just at this last digit. This lump is from by the constant pressure of gripping a pen between the thumb and first two fingers. You will never find it upon any but the most devoted writers and they will never be found without it."

"Also observe the discoloration at the tip of the index finger gentlemen, that is from dipping the tip of a pen into the open top of an inkwell. That it still remains so visible despite all the washings with this powerful disinfectant, is proof that the stain was indeed a dark one."

"Incredible," the Inspector said.

"The poor vision can be attested to by the well-set indentations upon both sides of the nose, just where glasses or pince-nez would have set.[24]

---

[23] "Third Molars" – the archaic term for wisdom teeth.

[24] Pince-nez – eyeglasses without earpieces. From the French term for pinched nose, from the pressure used to stay on. They reached their greatest popularity between 1880 and 1900.

"But I see no such indentations Mr. 'Olmes," someone challenged.

"No," Holmes replied, patiently. "The woman's flesh has swollen slightly but the indentations are quite obvious to the touch."

"If they are invisible, then why did you check?"

"As I've often told my friend, Dr. Watson here," Holmes said, smiling, "I expected to find them and, as you will learn, an examination is not complete without checking for such things, even when they are not apparent."

"The accompanying dimples found behind each ear also indicate that she wore glasses and of the type with the accompanying earpieces, rather than the more popular pince-nez."

Moving down to the victim's feet my friend pointed to the presence of highly developed bony bumps along the inside of both feet and at the base of the big toe.

"With such an acute case of bunions it would have been impossible for this young woman to engage in running or even in walking any great distance. The pain would have been…severe."

"So she hired on as someone's secretary."

"That is the logical conclusion based upon the facts at hand, however, it is possible that she may have been hired for a number of other sedentary jobs Inspector Redgrave. Further investigation is needed to determine what that might have been for certain and where.

The men erupted in a spontaneous chorus of clapping which, in short order, brought Inspector Lestrade to look in unhappily from the door.

"Alright lads," Redgrave said, "we've lauded Mr. Holmes enough for the present so let us move on with our own duties now. If you will follow me to the office Gentlemen."

"Is that where you found him?" Holmes asked.

"Mr. Holmes," the Inspector growled, spinning upon his heel and facing both of us in the lantern light, "if you'd lived in past ages Sir, I very much fear that old Spanish Inquisitors would've done for you."

"You can see them burning me happily upon the stake can you Inspector Redgrave? It may be just as well that I wasn't born then, for I would hate to put your theory to the test. Although by the look on Lestrade's face when we came in I don't doubt he'd gladly volunteer to strike the first match upon my pyre."

"Well you're correct enough about that, for he was sour grapes when he first heard my report," Redgrave said. "But back to this business, I was halfway across this room when the little, glassed-in office, just there, exploded with the blast of a pistol and the flash of the shot. I figured he'd seen the writing on the wall and knew the jig was up. After all he'd done, he knew it would be the rope sure and certain."

"So why prolong the agony," Holmes said.

"Just so Sir. He would have taken the easiest way out wouldn't he? There was a .476 caliber Army revolver laying on the floor next to his desk. I kept the men out so you could have first go. I've heard how you like that sort of thing."

"So no one has gone in?"

"No one and I've kept a man to see to that."

"Very well-done Inspector," Holmes remarked, "and when will we have more light?"

"I've sent for more lanterns but much of this place will remain invisible until morning if I'm right, and only then will we get a real good look at it. All the windows are covered in dust, even these interior office windows, as you can see, and I'll leave this lantern just for yourself."

Holmes took it with a nod and made his slow and painstaking entry into the room where the frozen face of Mr. Henry Fyldene, the Elder, hung back over the office chair and stared, wide-eyed, at the ceiling, as if he'd been trying to look into heaven itself.

"That is a horrific sight is it not Doctor?"

"It is indeed Inspector," I agreed, "unnatural."

"No matter how many of the dead I've come upon, I find I never get used to the thing. Do you suppose that will always be so?"

"It has been so for me I'm afraid," I confessed, as I watched my friend bend and move, adjusting the light in every conceivable angle to see into the corners and crevices.

"I've found death to be imbued with an infinite variety," Holmes commented, without pausing his search. "It is like birth in that way, it is always new, although you must appreciate that my experience with the former condition is far greater than it is with the latter one."

"Too much death and mores the pity Sir."

"I fear that death is the strong suit for every man in our line of work Inspector."

"That is a grim observation Mr. Holmes," the Inspector said, "And how about you Doctor?"

"What's that?" I asked.

"What about you Sir? Are you more familiar with birth or death?"

My life being with the Army had been set to come down upon the side of death long before I met Mr. Sherlock Holmes and my years since, working alongside the world's greatest detective, had added a closeness and acquaintanceship with death I could never have imagined.

"Death," I answered, "most definitely."

"I would have thought that birth would have promised a happier life," the Inspector proposed.

"I suppose," I replied, "but where would the world be without us Inspector Redgrave."

"There is that I suppose, but sometimes Doctor I feel we barely keep the lid on the whole thing."

Holmes continued his examination of the office as we turned to the timely arrival of a dozen more lanterns from Scotland Yard. For a full hour my friend stayed at the task before him in the office and then he rejoined us out in the surgery.

"What have you there?" Redgrave asked when Holmes emerged, gripping a sheet of paper.

"A sketch of the Tottenham Court Road victim Inspector, or someone very like her, and drawn by the woman herself if I'm not mistaken."

"How can you be so sure Holmes?" I enquired.

"Look at the wrist Watson," said he.

There upon the delicate wrist of the woman in the drawing...was the rose tattoo.

"Miss Rosenberg is it then?"

"Miss Tereza Amalia Rosenberg," Holmes said.

His words shocked us to no end and we stared at him in wonder.

"Henry Fyldene kept impeccable files upon his victims," my friend continued, pointing his thumb back toward the office. "All the paperwork is in there, including copies of their correspondence."

"Even their sketches?" I asked.

"Everything," Holmes said, sadly. "Their lives, just beginning, it's all there to see."

"Then we'll find out where each is from?" the Inspector exclaimed.

"Addresses, sketchbooks, family photographs, diaries, and even personal letters, they're all there Inspector Redgrave."

The Inspector excused himself and with the lantern and several men in tow, made his way to the office, leaving us momentarily to ourselves.

Henry Fyldene

"And Fyldene," I said, quietly.
"A .476 Eley to the roof of the mouth."[25]

---

[25] The .476 Eley was also known as the .476 Enfield, a British centrefire Army revolver.

"Then he knew you'd seen something in him?" I said, "for he certainly wasn't taken by surprise when Redgrave and his men came upon him."

"I believe you're right Watson. As you said, I do have a reputation."

"Why not flee though? He might've made an escape. You said it yourself Holmes, the man was a world traveler, spoke several languages..."

"Henry Fyldene, the Elder, was not a notable man Watson. Despite his wife's generous spirit and her defense of his career. No doubt she was fueled with notions of making something of the man in their early years and no doubt she tried hard to do it. What he did achieve must be laid fully at her feet, of that I have no doubt. It could not have been an easy task and there can be little doubt that, with the passing of years, she realized she'd made a mistake in marrying him, but it was done and what was she to do? Is it any wonder the poor woman suffered a misstep or two."

"So he lacked the wherewithal to attempt an escape?"

"He was a common enough little man who, as Mrs. Fyldene so deftly put it, knew he had the most excellent reasons for feeling insecure. Not just in his marriage either, but also in his career, where he found several older men of true genius, like Rawlinson. Had Fyldene been free to marry a woman from the nearby village and spend his days inventorying gloves and handkerchiefs in a local shop or selling supplies to the farms, he might've found a little happiness."

"But he was a Fyldene!" I remarked.

"A Fyldene with aspiring parents who dreamed of his *marrying up*," Holmes added, "and Elizabeth Osborne, a cousin to the Queen, that would have been a heady thing for them all."

"But instead of receiving every benefit from such a position, he was destined to mediocrity, misery, and bitterness."

"How did his wife put it, 'my poor Henry placed himself in a position where he could never achieve or acquire enough to feel secure in himself.' That was it my good fellow. It wasn't much as lives go but he had a rare woman Watson. And I don't speak only of her outward beauty. If he could only have realized it."

"She described his life a kind of *purgatory*," I said, recalling the sadness in her azure eyes.

"So here was a man with a mediocre career, betrayed in his marriage, and disappointed in his expectations, and he turned to prey upon the very people his experience had taught him were the most vulnerable and unprotected."

"Immigrants."

"Young immigrant women to be exact Watson, coming unescorted to a new country and full of hope for a brighter future," Holmes replied.

"They'd left the safety and protection of their own families and countries behind," I noted, "and were given no chance to establish themselves under the protection of the new. As you pointed out, they would not be missed."

"And their cases would be impossible to track. They were the perfect victims for a devil who realized he could never achieve anything close to the shining dreams his parents had set for him."

"Then his greatest achievement was gaining the hand of Elizabeth Osborne and that came early in his life," I observed.

"It was followed by a long and undistinguished career guaranteed to highlight his insignificance. The joy that offset this disappointing side of the ledger, the birth of his first son and namesake, turned in time the greatest disappointment and heartbreak of all."

"When he realized that his wife had been unfaithful to him," I said.

"And that the boy he had taken such pride in and placed such hope in, was not even his. His shame was magnified, if such a thing is even imaginable, when he grasped the fact that his wife's lover was obviously one of the Arabian men of their acquaintance."

"Holmes," I cried, "can you mean it?"

"You hadn't realized?" said he. "The boy was dark skinned, the couple was posted to Ottoman Arabia, and that was where she conceived."

"So it holds that the father was a native from that area."

"Fyldene's name never appeared in reports, his promotions were slow to come and inevitably disappointing, and he never received any of the coveted titles and rewards which were handed out so freely to those around him at the time. Then, after all this, he discovered that he had been a cuckold and a laughingstock, pouring his hopes and affections into another man's child.[26] All while it was all inescapably obvious to everyone who knew him."

"You've just described the most impossible position imaginable Holmes."

"It doesn't justify his actions, but it was this combination of critical factors, along with the sudden death of his father and the unavoidable alienation which followed with his wife and son, which brought about his first crimes."

"In September of '73?"

"Precisely and after the success of that atrocity, again in June of '74."

"He found that he could succeed at something, however wrong and wicked," I said.

"And the manner by which he conducted these crimes demonstrates the pride and satisfaction he derived from them Watson. The records he kept, even the clothing of each of the young women which he organized. Look at this if you would Watson but be warned that it is ghoulish."

---

[26] A cuckold is a man who unknowingly raises a child who is the offspring of the union of his wife with another man.

Holmes removed something from beneath his coat and laid it down upon the table, then lit a match and shielded it so that I could see the thing plainly. It was a frame and inside was a foreign word I didn't recognize.

"What does it say and is this leather?" I asked.

"It says Rosenberg," Holmes replied, "in the Czech language."

Only then did I realize that this was the skin of the young woman Fyldene had murdered, and this was the remainder of her tattoo. The man had put it in a tiny frame and displayed it in his office.

I jumped back, horrified.

"I apologize, I should have warned you rather than springing it upon you in that way."

"Holmes," I cried, "what kind of monster was this man?"

"The worst kind I'm afraid my good fellow, a weak one. The weak man, and insecure, is always the most brutal and vicious. He knows no bounds and mistreats those who come under his power. The man of character meanwhile, treats his fellow man civilly, whether in war or peace. There are lines he will not cross and things he will never do."

I stared in disbelief as the match burned out and Holmes crushed it beneath his shoe.

"You are shaken Watson?"

"Indeed I am," I muttered, looking toward the doorway. "It is that innocent young woman's own skin after all."

"Yes and she had those words placed there when she was a young girl."

"That's why the authorities only found the rose," I said.

"You are seeing it clearly," Holmes nodded.

"That's why he cut this portion off, because all along he intended on framing it as some foul memento to his sickness."

"Actually Watson, he removed this because it would've provided the police with the young woman's identity and country of origin and would have illuminated his modus operandi, but you're right about his sickness and the memento."

"This is human skin Holmes," I stammered out. "Have we ever seen more evil creature? I can think of none."

"They exist my good fellow, they certainly do," said he, removing the framed object from my sight. "In the grand scheme and balance of life Watson, I suspect that every time a man like you is born, it is offset by the cosmos with the birth of a man like Henry Fyldene, the Elder."

"As Inspector Redgrave likes to say, that is a grim thought."

"That is true my friend, but if it is grim it speaks to the desperate need the world has for every good man to do his part, for evil certainly will."

J. B. Varney

Chapter 6 – The Consulting Detective

We called at Ashburn House the next morning to confirm Holmes' views he said, but I suspected that there might be more to it than that.

"She will see us," my friend told the footman, imperiously. We'd just seen the man the previous day, when he had assigned us to the salon then went to inform his late master of our arrival.

"We'll wait in here," Holmes said, pointing with his walking stick to the salon.

The man was nothing without the backing of his employer and he shuffled off submissively without a single word of resistance.

I took the opportunity to examine the family portrait my friend had pinned so much on and this time I could see everything Holmes had pointed out. That anyone could have overlooked the clear evidence presented by the thing was unthinkable, although I had done just that the day before. Holmes had described the phenomenon to me, saying that the eyes see what the mind expects to see. I had expected to see the portrait of the Fyldene family, and so I did. My mind had glossed over the incongruities and I went about my business without the least disturbance. Now, however, I found it impossible not to notice the obvious facts presented by the picture.

"Mr. Holmes, Dr. Watson, have you any news?"

Mrs. Fyldene was now in mourning and dressed all in black, but she made no reference to the death of her husband or his heinous crimes.

"I'm afraid we must discuss another matter before I am able to proceed along that line," my friend said, from his place in front of the mantel.

"If you refer to my husband…"

"I do not Mrs. Fyldene, although you have our condolences."

"Yes," I added, "our sincerest condolences."

"Thank you both. My husband…nothing can be said to redeem his memory now. As to the pain he caused to so many innocent people…I can only grieve, but you said it was not about him that you called."

"I don't like to have mysteries at both ends of a case Mrs. Fyldene. Dr. Watson here can attest to this fact."

I nodded in confirmation of Holmes' statement.

"You, however, have presented me precisely with a case which has mysteries at both ends."

With this Holmes picked up the family portrait from the piano and placed it upon the mantle next to him.

"I don't understand," the poor woman said.

"You told me that you could think of no reason for your son's disappearance, but that was a lie wasn't it? I won't debate the matter with you," Holmes declared emphatically, "but neither will I continue with a case which is not fully disclosed."

The woman dropped into a chair, defeated, and hung her head, but she remained silent.

Holmes took up the family portrait again and handed it to me.

I now knew full well what he was referring to and I had no doubt that Mrs. Fyldene did also. Finally she took a deep breath and began.

"We were young Mr. Holmes and in love," she barely whispered, "and for a moment the whole world seemed ready to change for us. My husband was cold and distant, troubled by his bungling and mistakes, and he was always away. *He*, on the other hand, was utterly different."

The way she had pronounced the "he" made it clear she spoke of someone else, another man, and not her husband.

"He was from the desert, a son and soldier, and was so rash and brave. I won't try to excuse our love, for from one place it seems all madness and folly, doomed from the outset. But I will say that we were married according to the custom of his people and yes gentlemen, I bore him a son, a beautiful, noble son, my Henry. My precious boy."

She had not looked up and Holmes signaled me to remain silent despite her pause.

"He was from the Najd, the vast desert heart of Ottoman Arabia, and his tribe was both a desert and a horse people. His name was Abdul and we met in Meccah where my husband had been posted, at an official dinner."

"Henry was called away to distant Bagdad in the north," she continued, "and our friendship grew into something *more*. I already spoke Arabic and I easily learned Abdul's dialect. We shared many hopes for the future. I have two sons, each from a different father, and I tell myself that I love them equally Mr. Holmes. I tell others as well; in the hope it will help me believe the lie."

I saw from the glint in Holmes' eyes that he understood the woman's statement and her dilemma, but he said nothing.

"But to be honest, one is the son of my love and the other is the son of my duty. You demanded to know all this Mr. Holmes and now you can see for yourself that it has nothing to do with my son's disappearance."

"How can you be so sure Mrs. Fyldene?"

"Because I know Abdul and he could never hurt his own son."

"And your youngest son?" I asked, curiously.

"Alfred is away at school, thank God, and I will make sure that he has as little knowledge of the nightmare I now find myself in as is possible. I will protect him."

"Have you remained in contact with *Abdul* over the years?" Holmes asked.

"I couldn't risk such a *luxury* once we were moved permanently to Bagdad. Our son was just two at that time so he has no memory at all...of his father."

"Of his real father?" my friend clarified.

"Yes, of his real father."

"But your son had to feel the change in your husband's behavior," I remarked, "when..."

"When he discovered my *indiscretion* Doctor?"

"Yes, when he discovered your indiscretion, for no man could mask such a disappointment and shock even from a child."

"My son was almost fifteen when my husband finally realized the truth. The only kindness was that my son was away at school much of the year."

"I say it again Mrs. Fyldene, your eldest son had to feel the loss of his father's affections toward him. Your husband could not have disguised his sentiments even if he had desired to do so and, as you know, he had no reason to do that."

"The discovery that young Henry was the son of another man nearly destroyed my husband," said she, "and it did destroy our marriage Mr. Holmes. Although we've stayed together it was all for appearances, we were husband and wife in name only after that terrible time. What I am about to say may seem impossible for you to accept, but it is a testament to a son's love that young Henry did not take notice of his father's change at first, and not for nearly a year after. As a father, my husband had always favored little Alfred. I sometimes wondered if it wasn't in the nature of our species, which naturally drew a man to his true son more than to a false son. My dear Henry had grown up with the sad knowledge that his father loved his brother more. It took him some time to finally admit the complete loss of his father's affections."

e   "What did you tell him when the time came?"

"I told him the truth, although God knows I didn't want to. He was after all only a boy at the time and I knew how he looked up to me. I would have much preferred to wait, for his sake."

"And for yours?" Holmes asked.

"I suppose so, but I knew that my husband, in his anger, would lash out at some point and the truth would then come spilling out without care."

"How did young Henry react to your news?"

"He was, of course, shocked, for he had idolized me despite all my faults, and he'd never dreamt that Henry might not be his father even if Alfred was his favorite. The coldness that then came to exist between the two of them was hard to live with, especially for me and Alfred. All semblance of a loving family was then lost forever."

"So when this family portrait was taken…"

"Yes Dr. Watson, when that portrait was taken young Henry was aware that my husband was not his father."

"And you never contacted…the Arabian, not even after your husband discovered your secret? After all, you are married to the man *according to his custom*," my friend said, brusquely.

"I have never again seen or written to Abdul and he undoubtedly has married several women during his life, as is also their custom, and has had many other sons. I had my life in England and could see nothing to be gained for either of us by opening that door again."

"And what about your son? Did he not want to meet his true father?"

"He was content to hear my descriptions and to have a daguerreotype of Abdul to look at. The two share a remarkable likeness."

"Did you notice any change in your eldest son's manner or behavior after that? Or did he speak to you of any desire to visit his real father?"

"He was able to be at peace with my husband's coldness after that, but in short order he was away at college and very much occupied. When he returned to London he always stayed at his club, even though we kept his rooms here for him."

"Which club?" Holmes asked, "The Oxford & Cambridge Club?"

"That's right Mr. Holmes, at 71 Pall Mall."

"And he avoided your husband."

"He was able to avoid him almost completely. It was a state of things which was agreeable to both men Mr. Holmes; I can assure you."

"Did this not rob you and your youngest son of the other's company?" I asked.

"It did of course Dr. Watson, but we met when we could, just the three of us. Sometimes we'd have lunch at Henry's club and other times we would meet at one of the galleries or museums for the afternoon. Once we were able to get away for one of Henry's races. It was not ideal but it was far better than the constant tension. Obviously, once young Henry realized that Alfred was only his half-brother, there was something lost between them too. I'm afraid my failure cost them far more than I ever imagined could be possible."

"So Alfred knows too?" I probed. "About your indiscretion and his brother."

"No, these last years he has known that there was some trouble between his father and brother and he is very aware that he has always been his father's favorite. My husband would call Alfred his 'Little Man,' and show him every preference imaginable, but I am quite sure that he has never guessed the truth about his brother."

"Difficult times for you Mrs. Fyldene," Holmes remarked, showing some care for the first time.

"And difficult days ahead, once these crimes are laid at my husband's door, but I still pray you will find my son Mr. Holmes, now that I've told you everything, and then my sons and I will get through this together as best we can."

"We will visit Miss Waldron," Holmes offered, bringing an end to our interview, "and then we will go to the Oxford & Cambridge Club on Pall Mall. Who shall I ask for?"

"Mr. Stevens can show you to Henry's room."

"Thank you Mrs. Fyldene," I said, but she acted as if she hadn't heard me.

"Before you go gentlemen, there is something I must say."

We both looked respectfully upon the woman who had born up under so much tribulation for so many years. I did not excuse her actions but I also could not ignore the price she and her children had paid. This was to say nothing of what they would pay in the future as well, as a result of Henry Fyldene's crimes.

"I can't pretend to mourn my husband before you men, now that the truth is known, but I do mourn the young women he murdered."

Henry Fyldene

"That is a noble sentiment," I remarked.

"I can do nothing for their families but I have two sons and I know how stricken I would be if anything happened to either of them. So I ask you to bring my Henry back to me, Mr. Holmes."

"What a rare and beautiful woman she is," I said, once we were settled in our cab and bound for the home of Miss Marianne Waldron.

Holmes smiled at my words.

"You have always been a most appreciative admirer of the fair sex Watson."

"I know that you recognize beauty as much as I do Holmes, despite your usual silence."

"Oh I do my good fellow, I do. It's just that the most beautiful woman I've ever known poisoned a husband, a suitor, and an employer, and, if she had not been stopped, she would most definitely have continued upon her murderous path."

"Surely that is an exception to the rule."

"Of course she was an exception, for the vast majority of women never commit murder, but the moral, that the outward appearance is a most dangerous method of judging others, must not be missed my good fellow."

"So I shouldn't judge the book by the cover."

"That is correct, for that proverb is the result of ages of observation and painful experience."

It didn't take long to get to 68 St. James, it being just beyond James Lock & Co., Hatters, where Holmes and I purchased most of our head gear.

Henry Fyldene

The four-story greystone of the Waldron's was architecturally a surprisingly plain Italianate, but it was exquisitely appointed indoors and we were shown into Miss Marianne Waldron in the library. Compared with the treatment we'd first received from the Fyldene's footman at Ashburn House, the Waldron's footman treated us with an excess of civility and decorum.

"I am reading 'Pride and Prejudice' just now," said the young lady, rising and offering us her hand.[27] "Although to be strictly correct I should say that I am reading it again, just now, for I have enjoyed it several times."

"I read it once myself," I offered.

"And how did you find the book Dr. Watson? Was it not...divine?"

"It was...most entertaining," I admitted.

After Holmes' cautionary tale regarding the most beautiful woman of his experience, I was slower to declare the young woman attractive and remarkable, at least in the privacy of my own mind. Instead I watched her throughout our interview and, in the end, settled upon a more sober judgment, that she was a precocious young lady of romantic sensibilities, and quite lovely.

Holmes explained our purpose in visiting and our commission from Mrs. Fyldene and the young woman rose and opened one of the bookcases.

---

[27] Pride and Prejudice, by Jane Austen, published 1813.

"I have a few dates here which might be of use to you Mr. Holmes," said she, in a businesslike fashion. "They will at least provide you with some general idea of Henry's movements leading up to the day of his disappearance."

She then withdrew a leatherbound journal from the bookcase, closed the glass cabinet door, and returned to her chair.

She flipped rapidly through the pages in the manner of someone who is very familiar with the entries and locations.

"Here we are gentlemen. It was three weeks ago, nearing the last week of October."

"I beg your pardon," Holmes said, "but am I to infer that this journal is a record of young Mr. Fyldene's movements?"

"Henry is an important part of my world so it follows that he would play a large part in my diary Mr. Holmes."

"Very logical," I replied, supportively.

"It was on the fifteenth of October when he was first late for tea, by nearly an half an hour, and first spoke the name of Freddy Capshaw in my company. I remember because I considered the latter to be the cause of the former's tardiness."

"A school chum perhaps," I offered.

"A Cambridge boy," she said, disapprovingly.

"This *tardiness*," Holmes enquired.

"Henry had never been late to our tea times prior to his mention of Mr. Freddy Capshaw."

"You gentlemen may think it a silly thing, but I placed great significance upon this connection."

"And rightly so," Holmes replied, impressed by the young lady's logic. "It is a rare thing for a person to think so clearly," said he, "and it is also rare for a young man to be so punctual."

"Not when it has to do with the love of his life," Miss Waldron replied.

"That is what he calls you?" I asked.

"No," she admitted, "he hasn't worked up the nerve yet, but he will. Still he is never late."

"October 15th," Holmes repeated, writing it down in his notebook, "late by thirty minutes and mentioned Freddy Capshaw, a Cambridge boy."

"That's correct Mr. Holmes and on the 18th we were to meet at Verey's in Regent Street for a special dinner, but Henry never appeared. It is a most fortunate thing for me that it is now acceptable for young women to go out even while unaccompanied by a man or I would have felt most scandalous indeed gentlemen."

"Indeed," Holmes empathized, "but what did Mr. Fyldene say by way of his defense?"

"Nothing at all Mr. Holmes, although I asked him four times. It was quite enough to make me suspicious that there was another woman in his life, at least until he proposed."

With this she held out her hand and showed an exquisite golden engagement ring with a lustrous opal setting.

"Congratulations," I offered sincerely.

She beamed proudly in response and blushed.

"And this was on the 18th?" Holmes asked.

"No Sir. Henry missed our dinner on the 18th. He proposed upon the 21st, here in our salon and he was dashingly gallant upon one knee."

This last bit of information, while of no obvious importance to our investigation, provided the young lady with a good deal of satisfaction. I had heard that a woman went up substantially in the eyes of her lady friends, if she could report that her intended had proposed *upon one knee*."

"And was he prompt upon that date?"

"Yes, early in fact, which was like him."

"And he went missing when? The 24th?"

"The evening of the 25th Mr. Holmes. We were to meet at the Albion, as their rooms are so dazzling you know, to celebrate our engagement."

"And he'd been seen earlier in the day?"

"Mr. Stevens, the keeper at his club. He had talked with Henry and noted his enthusiasm regarding the evening's plans."

"But no notes or messages were received to explain this absence either?"

"Nothing Mr. Holmes and I was quite upset by it by this time, as it was a repeat of his earlier folly. Now I only pray you can find him."

"And this Freddy Capshaw, how was it he became the subject of your conversation?"

"Henry said the man was a most daring and successful cricketer and hoped we'd be able to watch him play in the coming season."

"I think I've heard of this Capshaw fellow," I said to Holmes. "I believe he is a first-rate leg spinner. You say he is from Cambridge?"[28]

"That's right Doctor and Henry just finished at Oxford, but he talked about the man as if they were the best of chums."

---

[28] Leg-Spinner – a type of bowling (pitching) used in cricket.

"Is there anything else you would like to draw our attention to Miss Waldron? Anything out of the ordinary for instance."

"Besides his tardiness and the absences, and not answering my questions, although I did ask four times. I don't think so. He did seem distracted though, which goes without saying I suppose."

Before we took our leave Holmes praised the young woman's journal and repeated how rare it was to have precise information.

The Pall Mall façade of the Oxford & Cambridge Club rose 75 feet up and was set off by a dramatic portico complete with Corinthian Columns.

The arms of the venerable universities hung upon the columns nearest the main doors and made an impressive show up and down the broad boulevard.

"It is an honor to meet you Mr. Holmes," Mr. Stevens declared, earnestly, "and you as well Dr. Watson. My family reads your stories regularly though we never get enough of them. Not that I'm complaining Sir, I'm sure. You are *busy* no doubt."

The crisp little man declared his concern for the missing Henry Fyldene as he showed us to the latter's apartment on an upper floor. Before he could excuse himself, however, Holmes asked about the Capshaw fellow.

"A recent arrival and a likable gentleman. I did notice him often in the company of Mr. Fyldene."

Fyldene's apartment was made up of a small but airy sitting room with two large windows looking down upon Pall Mall and supplying a wealth of natural light, a comfortably appointed bedroom with double bed, and a small bathroom with a shower. Larger and smaller apartments were available for members, at respective prices.

I stood in the entry hall while Holmes went about his routine and a short time into it I was accosted by a dapper young man with dark features. He was not unlike the image of Henry Fyldene himself, which I'd seen in the family portrait at Ashburn House.

"You must be the detectives," he said, looking past me in the obvious hope of getting a glimpse of the famous consulting detective, Mr. Sherlock Holmes.

"His mother told me she'd placed all her hope in two stellar fellows of good repute. You are quite the vogue now and I will be a regular celebrity when I tell my friends about meeting you."

"May I ask your name?" I said.

"Frederick Betancort Capshaw at your service, but you can call me Freddy. Everyone does."

"Mr. Capshaw to see you," I called, knowing Holmes would want to interrogate the fellow.

"Bring him straight in if you will Watson.

I led the man in but found the room oddly empty. Only then did my friend show himself from behind the sofa as a smile played about his lips.

With a single, graceful bound he leaped up and over the sofa and landed silently in the center of the sitting room, where he took a bow.

"Sherlock Holmes," said he, "a pleasure." Then, before the young man could utter a single word Holmes motioned him to a chair and took a seat himself in a nearby wingback.

"You're a recent acquaintance of Mr. Fyldene, I believe I've heard."

"You are dashed well informed Mr. Holmes."

"And when did you become acquainted?"

"A few weeks back," said he, candidly. "We found we had some things in common and hit it off from the start, despite us being bitter rivals you know. I'm from Cambridge and Henry was a dyed-in-the-wool Oxford Blue or Dark Blue, if you know what I mean."

"And Cambridge is the Light Blue, I believe," said I, "speaking of the rival schools."

"Yes that's true enough, but most people don't know that the colors for both schools, the dark blue and the light blue, originated at Eton.

"What sort of things did you have in common?"

"Well look at me Mr. Holmes, I can't hide it you know? If you've seen Henry you've pretty much seen me. We're both moderns of course, you can see that much, and we've both got parents from different races. Most people are too polite to use the vulgar terms for us, at least to our faces. My mum was from the Araby, God rest her soul, and my father is as proud an Englishman as you'll ever find.[29] Henry's father is from somewhere over there too, the Araby I think, some sheik or sultan or something, and his mum is from some regal English family, so there was that. Then we're both athletes. He was a dashed good rower for the Oxford Blue, as you probably know.[30] And I'm a Cambridge cricketer and fairly good some say."

"So you two hit it off?" Holmes asked.

"Sure did and we both enjoyed talking. The gift of the gab I guess. Some of the *other fellows* are a

---

[29] Araby or The Araby, archaic term for the Arabian world.
[30] The official color of the Cambridge University Boat Club.

fairly tight-lipped bunch, that stiff-upper-lip sort of nonsense. I mean if you ask me. No offense meant gentleman, I'm sure."

"What did you mean Mr. Capshaw," I asked, "when you said you were both 'moderns'?"

"Henry and I didn't get too involved in the old ways and customs on either side or our families, we'd both chosen to be, more-or-less, exactly what we are really."

"Modern men?" Holmes said.

"That's right Mr. Holmes, like you always say in your stories, we are men of science too."

"And you are the son of the Captain Capshaw who commanded the good ship 'Archimedes' safely through the Great Atlantic Storm back in June of '58?"[31]

"I say Mr. Holmes, that's dashed impressive, but the old guvnor packed it in shortly after that I'm afraid. He said no one lives through two such storms in one lifetime and so called it quits."[32]

"And you are still in college?"

"I'll finish up next June, if I'm lucky," the young man said, jokingly, for everyone knew it took far more than luck to pass Cambridge.

"Do you engage in any business on the side," Holmes enquired, "perhaps in preparation of your graduation."

---

[31] Two ships laying the first Atlantic telegraph cable weathered the same storm in 1858.

[32] Guvnor – Victorian term for an authority: father, boss, etc.

"No Sir, the good old guvnor sees to my all needs with a regular, if modest, allowance, so that I may concentrate upon my studies."

"And on cricket," I added.

"That too Dr. Watson."

Chapter 7 – The Stars Align

"I've contacted Godfrey Broughton, Esquire, Watson," Holmes said, from the comfort of his old chair once we were back in Baker Street. "He is the boon companion of our missing man. While we await him I wonder if you would not share your thoughts on this morning's interviews with me."

"I don't know what I have to offer," I replied, somewhat put out by my friend's treatment of Mrs. Elizabeth Fyldene.

"I must say that you habitually underestimate yourself my good fellow. Your thoughts have often proven illustrative to me and did you not impress the good inspector just recently."

"Well then," I said, "I feel I must point out that you were more than a little hard on Mrs. Fyldene. Under the circumstances some sympathy would have been justified."

"Hard?" said he, in response.

"Churlish then," I responded, but when my friend's face remained unchanged I said, "surly."

He shook his head.

"You cannot be ignorant of the fact that the death of Mrs. Fyldene's husband can come only as a relief to her after all she has endured, can you?"

"There is her missing son to be considered and then the stain of the crimes upon the name."

"You are a true nobleman Watson and no one who knows you will ever be in doubt of that fact. As to this woman, however, I'm afraid you have made a misstep."

"A misstep?"

"You'll admit it is a kinder word than blunder."

"So I've blundered in wishing some sympathy for Mrs. Elizabeth Fyldene?"

"Even you cannot deny that she knowingly kept crucial information from us in this case."

"About the young man's parentage?"

"Indeed and are we simply to overlook that fact now, because this was the beautiful and elegant Elizabeth Fyldene, after demanding honesty upon principle from every other client we've had?"

"But it has no bearing upon his disappearance!"

"No bearing? My good fellow, how is it possible for you to make such a declaration at this point?"

"That his father is some desert sheik! Do you really believe that fact is vital to this case? Or that the man, who Mrs. Fyldene herself said likely has a great many other sons, has come around the world because of loneliness or sentimentality, to seize upon this one? No Holmes, it was a private secret to which the woman attached great shame and it had nothing to do with the disappearance of her son. It should have been left undisturbed. I cannot condemn her for trying to keep it private and I don't believe that a *gentleman* would have forced it out as you did."

It was not the first time I'd reproved my friend, for he could be gallingly unfeeling at times, but as Mrs. Fyldene's secret was so clearly peripheral to the case, I found his behavior unacceptable.

"You are most outspoken in your feelings my good fellow," said he, quietly, as his eyes moved toward the fire.

"As you asked me to share my thoughts..."

"On the morning's interviews," said he, "not upon the propriety of my approach with...*her*."

"I believed it important."

"And if you honestly believe that her *secret* has no part in the disappearance of her son, then I must say that you are mistaken my friend."

After this declaration, which I found shocking to say the least, he rose and went to his room.

Time passed with the only sound the ticking clock to keep me company as I walked up and down the room and stared aimlessly out upon a bleak and overcast Baker Street, with barely a trickle its usual traffic.

Holmes had been pursuing the facts of the case from the beginning, as he invariably did. He was the compass needle when the game was afoot and as a sleuthhound he'd never failed to follow the scent wherever it led. I had...*blundered*.

An interminable hour and a half passed in this way before the pull at our bell announced the arrival of Mr. Godfrey Broughton, Esquire.

As Holmes didn't emerge, I received our young visitor when he arrived.

"A summons from Mr. Sherlock Holmes is not something one receives every day," the young man said, handing me over his coat and hat.

"No indeed," Holmes replied, standing in his doorway, "nor is the presence of a Broughton in the sitting room of 221 B Baker Street."

"You flatter me Sir and my old father would gladly enlighten you regarding any number of my many shortcomings, I'm sure."

"Yet you are destined to be a chancellor of the Exchequer or a Prime Minister no less."

"I would give a great deal to eavesdrop upon a conversation between you and my father Sir," Mr. Broughton said as he and Holmes shook hands, "were such a thing not so uncouth."

"No doubt you have your own particular views of your father as well. It is ever the way of things."

The young gentleman nodded in agreement with Holmes and accepted a cup of tea and plate of Mrs. Hudson's cucumber sandwiches.

"Thank you Dr. Watson."

"The sandwiches are a house specialty of our landlady," Holmes said, graciously.

"I am as devastated by the disappearance of poor Henry as anyone could be," Broughton said, without even a preamble. "I cannot shake the thought of him...somewhere, suffering. I saw him the day before he vanished. We met at the Criterion to catch up."

"And did he give you any idea of what he was involved with?"

"He told me he'd been practicing with some of the other Blues who live down here in London. You knew he was a first rate 8-rower didn't you?"

"I was aware he rowed for Oxford," Holmes replied, knowing little about the sport.

"The 7 and 8-rowers set the stroke rate and rhythm for the whole crew, so Henry played an important role. He was one of the best to come out of Oxford Mr. Holmes and there was even talk of him going back to coach the Blue."

"So this was the topic of your conversation?"

"That and he told me he'd finally proposed to Miss Waldron of St. James Street. He's been head over heels since he first met the girl, although he was quite sure she had no clue how desperate he was to gain her hand in marriage."

"Then it was a noteworthy day for him?"

"Rather a hopeless case," said Broughton, with a toss of his head and a hearty laugh.

"You are not a fan of marriage Mr. Broughton?" I enquired.

"I don't have anything against it Dr. Watson, if that's what you mean, but it does seem to be the miracle cure for happiness doesn't it?"

"Then you are not a romantic?" Holmes asked.

"I'm speaking now as a witness and a realist Mr. Holmes, for I've not seen five truly happy couples left in a hundred and that after just five years. The numbers drop off precipitously thereafter. Long odds against happiness, that's my view of it."

"But your friend Henry was happy enough to enter into matrimony?"

"Actually he seemed more relieved to have the girl's answer than anything. I wouldn't have said he was excited, at least not as I'd expected, not for all the build-up if you know what I mean."

"I think I do Mr. Broughton, but if I were to ask you if you felt this new chum of Henry's was a good influence, what would you say?"

"You'd be speaking of Capshaw, the Cricketer."

"Frederick Betancort Capshaw," Holmes said.

"Yes, I met him just the once. It was at a dinner at the London Bar. I couldn't help notice how taken with the fellow Henry was and they both had...that similar look, if you know what I mean, so I guess it was natural enough."

"Yes but what did you think of Mr. Capshaw?"

"I can't say I trusted the fellow even if Henry was pleased to introduce his two best friends to each other, the old one in my case and the new one in Capshaw's. I went along with it but..."

"It's interesting that within so short a time of his befriending Capshaw, your friend vanishes. For all I can find Mr. Broughton, Henry told no one who was close to him what was happening."

Holmes' observation surprised me.

"You speak as if he knew what was coming Mr. Holmes, but I don't think he had any idea. I think someone was setting my friend up and now you point it out, it didn't take long once that Capshaw came into the picture did it?"

"And you haven't heard anything from Henry, not since the day before he vanished?"

"Actually, now that you ask about it, I received a note from him on the very evening of the day we met at the Criterion."

"By the post?" Holmes asked, excitedly.

"Just so."

"Then it was sent at least two days prior to your meeting at the Criterion," Holmes observed, "for nowhere in London is service faster than that at present, not for all the talk of reform. What were the contents?"

"That's just it Mr. Holmes. It was just a note. You know the sort of thing, 'doing fine, busy, blah, blah, blah. Twenty-five words or less, maybe."

"But no hint that he was about to ask the girl of his dreams to marry him?"

"Not a single word."

"Does that not strike you as a bit odd?" said he. "Especially as by the time he'd met with you at the Criterion he had already carried out the deed?"

"I say Mr. Holmes, that is peculiar isn't it?" Mr. Broughton replied. "By the way, you must tell your Landlady that these are uncommonly good little sandwiches."

After our guest's departure Holmes remained silent, still bothered by our *set to* earlier no doubt.

"I must apologize for my words," I said.

"Not at all my good fellow," said he, with a genuine cordiality and openness. "I confess that I am the most detached devil that ever went about in shoe leather Watson, and that must include even my own brother, Mycroft, which is saying something. When the mood is on me though, I can be most insensitive lout you've ever met. Your reproach was well-deserved and I am man enough to admit it. If you erred Watson, you erred upon the side of zeal and conviction and no one can declare the spirit of chivalry dead so long as you walk the earth my dear friend."

Holmes shocked me. He had a gift of doing what I least expected and for that I was thankful.

"Now," said he, reaching for his old black pipe and his Persian slipper, "let us look at what we've learned thus far."

"First off then, that Godfrey Charles Broughton, Esq., of the Broughton's of Otton Leigh, Granton, and Mayfair, can afford the finest things in London is only *logical*. On the other hand, how the son of Captain Capshaw, who is now pensioned off and living a quiet life in York, can have the financial wherewithal to appear in the role of a stylish young beau in a new gray suit from Savile Row no less, and with membership in the Oxford & Cambridge Club, is another thing altogether."

"That's right," I said, recalling the young man's earlier comment, "he said his father provided him only a modest allowance."

"And after paying for a Cambridge education it would have to be the very definition of modest."

"Certainly not Savile Row," I offered, "and not an apartment at the Oxford & Cambridge Club!"

"So there's the open question of where that young man is getting his money?" I said.

"And what is he doing to earn it Watson? I am having him followed even as we speak, so I hope we will soon know more," Holmes said. "Secondly there is strange case of Miss Marianne Waldron of 68 St. James Street to consider."

"What is that?" I asked.

"That the young man who was so eager to ask Miss Waldron to marry him, mentioned nothing of his plan just two days earlier when he sent his best friend the note."

"That is odd," I agreed, "and I cannot imagine anyone leaving such a momentous event to the spur of the moment."

"You're right Watson. Such times are invariably orchestrated and highly anticipated, especially among *that class*."

Holmes was himself of *that class* and yet he often spoke like someone looking in at customs and mores he had little understanding of.[33] It was just one of the many mysteries alive in my friend.

"What can be deduced from that?" I asked.

"The first thing that seems glaringly obvious is that Mr. Freddy Capshaw was the harbinger of this drama and that he had been commissioned to approach Henry Fyldene. The second item is that Fyldene was driven to distraction by whatever Capshaw was offering or…threatening. This drove his forgetfulness."

"That at least makes sense to me," I remarked.

"Third, that he expected to be plucked away at some fast-approaching but unknowable point, and very much wished to seal Miss Waldron into a commitment to him before that time."

"That seems logical, as he is head over heels for the girl," I observed, putting myself in the young man's shoes, "but it is still very much a mystery."

"Fourthly, that Capshaw first revealed his true purpose to Fyldene upon the 18th of October."

---

[33] Mores are the practices and customs which are accepted within a society, region, or social group.

"When he was to meet Miss Waldron at Verey's Restaurant for their special dinner."

"But Fyldene never appeared and, later, when he did, he would not explain what had happened."

"Even though she asked him four times," I said. "That must mean the answer was a terrible one!"

"And he only escaped censure by proposing."

"That was on the 21st."

"He was preparing for his departure then and was prompt about his business," Holmes said.

"So he knew he would be leaving?"

"He still didn't know the exact date, but he'd learned something from Capshaw that intimated it would be soon."

"Then he vanished on the evening of the 25th."

"And as far as we know Mr. Stevens at his club was the last of our witnesses to talk with him."

"Steven's saw that Fyldene was excited about the evening," I recalled, "but heard nothing of any significance to what ultimately occurred."

"Which implies that Fyldene still did not know he would be leaving that day, but he was notified sometime after his talk with Mr. Stevens. Then he vanished without a trace."

"But nothing has been received, either by his mother or his fiancé, no notes or messages."

"Which implies that Capshaw's deal with him, required that he forego any communications after his departure and Fyldene has complied, if he has any choice in the matter."

"But to what end Holmes?"

"Clearly to remove all possibility of pursuit or interruption. Whoever is behind this mystery is unwilling to risk imprisonment or perhaps worse, to have Mr. Fyldene's untrammeled attention."

"Then you know where the young man is?"

"Generally speaking Watson, I do, but as to specific location, not as yet."

"Is his life in danger?"

"I don't believe that Mr. Fyldene, even as young and inexperienced as he is, would have agreed to something which could have placed his life in danger. This is reinforced by the action he took to engage Miss Waldron prior to his disappearance. It is abundantly clear that he planned on returning and marrying the young woman."

"Could he have been deceived by Capshaw?"

"It is theoretically possible but it becomes less plausible with each hour that passes without a body. If he was deceived and his abductor's purpose was malevolent, surely something would have been seen, found, or heard by now?"

"Of course, it only makes sense. And you say it has something to do with his paternity?"

"The clues present a strong argument for that conclusion, although I admit it does sound most extraordinary. Yet the truth is often stranger than fiction and despite Mrs. Fyldene's assurances and your doubts, the clues tell this story."

"What assurances did she give?" I enquired.

Henry Fyldene

"That Henry Fyldene's real father has a great many other sons."

"And you have reason to doubt it?"

"If he does have a great many sons, then we are left to grapple with your peerless logic Watson. Then his reason for coming all the way around the world would have nothing to do with loneliness or sentimentality, those reasons you so confidently referred to earlier."

Even if it verged upon the unimaginable to think that a Bedouin tribesman from Arabia had indeed made his way to London to abduct his son, Holmes' reasoning was difficult to debate. His principle, which might almost be considered his refrain, argued that once the impossible was eliminated, whatever remained, no matter how improbable, must of necessity be the truth.

Even after all I'd seen, the fact that he'd made sense of the mystery thus far, based upon the testimony of a handful of witnesses, amazed me.

"And when will we find out where Capshaw went off to?"

"When there is something to know of course. The Irregulars are nothing if not thorough," said he, with obvious pride, "but it should be soon."

The afternoon wore on with no news from Holmes' streetwise eyes and ears and no visitors from Scotland Yard. My friend finally picked up his violin and treated me to a glorious concert which included some of his own compositions.

The barkers selling the evening edition soon could be heard declaring the shocking conclusion of the Tottenham Court Road Mystery. The people would have to buy a copy to learn that the killer had struck before, back in '73 and '74, but even before I read Holmes the articles from the Star and the Illustrated Police News, he already knew more than they did. It was ever the way of things when he was involved in the case being peddled upon the streets, but such was his nature that he still wanted to know what was being said.

"I say Holmes!" I exclaimed, as I got to the identity of the guilty man, "the killer wasn't Fyldene after all. Scotland Yard has laid the crime upon one Martin Hillblom. What is this?"

"A favor to me Watson," he said. "Lestrade and Redgrave took my request to their superiors and in light of my *contributions* in the past, they agreed to this sleight of hand. It is only temporary, however, and will come out in the morning."

"That gives Mrs. Fyldene a momentary reprieve from the horror yet to befall her family."

"The deception will also keep Henry Fyldene, the Younger, and whoever has him, in the dark regarding the truth of the case."

"To what end?"

"To keep from alerting those we pursue."

"Well it is an ugly business whatever name you give it," I replied.

"A grim chapter in our history, to be sure."

"Yes but successfully closed thanks to you."

Holmes remained silent.

"What would have come of things had Henry Fyldene, the Elder, simply avoided you when we went to his home?" I asked, curious now if it might have made a difference.

"The man's background," Holmes replied, "and the appearance of Catlin's books upon the North American Indians and human anatomy I saw in his salon, taken together, would no doubt have called to me."

"And it would have been enough?"

"You make an excellent point though Watson, as my focus on the disappearance of the younger Fyldene and the absence of any further clues regarding the elder, may well have proven enough to distract me from the Tottenham business."

"Then his gamble in choosing to confront you was foolish," said I.

"Certainly reckless, but your choice of the word *gamble* is an apt description. You will find that those who experience a consistent kind of success in some endeavor, whatever it be, inevitably begin to imagine themselves the *sole reason* for their success. This conclusion cannot help but fill them with confidence and often you'll find them making the most ill-advised decisions."

"But might it not be argued that their very success proves their genius?"

"Of course and a degree of success is indeed tied to their own genius in the moment, as you put it, or to their idea or concept, for example. What is sometimes identified as genius, however, can sometimes be little more than a highly developed eye for the *angle* Watson, what we know by the name opportunist. Our species finds it easy to forget that each of us is ever merely one factor in our success. To prove this, sometimes we succeed despite ourselves, at least for a season. When you credit all the factors in one's success, the humble man remains wisely cautious."

My skepticism must have been apparent to him for he continued.

"It could not be simpler to prove Watson, although it is just one example of thousands," said he. "We need not look beyond Bonaparte, for the invasion of Russia cannot be viewed in any light other than the most reckless of gambles. It might even be stated, mathematically, that beginning a war with a country of such vast proportions, in land mass, in natural resources, and with so great a population of compliant citizens, while already engaged with an enemy upon another front, was an act of undiluted stupidity."

"And no amount of genius can be expected to offset such outrageous decisions."

"It is worth consideration Watson, to question the intelligence of a man capable of overlooking so overwhelming a body of evidence in order to engage in such an assured folly. At some point we must conclude that a chain of unwise and reckless choices stems not from bad luck or fate, but from stupidity and hubris."

"Then the past successes begin to look more like luck than genius," I said, finally grasping my friend's point.

"Precisely Watson, and that vile opportunism which even a modest charlatan may possess in abundance, and that brings us back to Mr. Henry Fyldene, the Elder."

Chapter 8 – The Dead Diplomats

When Billy brought up the late edition of the Times, however, the headline was dominated for the moment, not with the sensational reports of the disappearance of Henry Fyldene or with the Torso Murders, but with news concerning the siege of Khartoum, in the Sudan, where General Gordon had been trapped for over six months.[34]

---

[34] The Siege of Khartoum, March 1884 through January 1885, was a major chapter in the Mahdist War (1881-1899). British

"Look here Holmes," I cried, excited, "one of Gordon's couriers has escaped from Khartoum, eluded the Mahdist Horde, and made it to Cairo with a satchel of official dispatches."

"What does it say Watson?"

"What Gladstone's government has allowed to be released to the press says that the situation in Khartoum is untenable. Of the thirty thousand inside the walls most are civilians and Gordon's spies estimate the Mahdist Army at nearly the same number, but that is all in desert warriors. The besieged are frantic," I said, sobered by the words I was reading, "as food supplies are nearly exhausted and hundreds have already died of starvation. Gordon reports that morale is low."

"And still the government drags its feet upon sending the relief column? Does it say anything about that?" Holmes demanded.

"No," I replied, flatly, "there is not a word."

"I am thankful you are not there Watson," he said, staring fiercely into the flames.

"Surely Gladstone won't see them abandoned to the zealots," I remarked, mainly to myself.

"The Prime Minister committed to their relief under obvious duress Watson, in July," Holmes reminded. "It is now November and with no sign of the least movement."

Army officer Charles George Gordon was made Governor-General of Sudan, a part of the British protectorate of Egypt.

"They required French-Canadian boatmen," I said, repeating the official line, "to get their boats up the Nile."

"Four months already gone my good fellow, waiting for French-Canadian boatmen! You are a stalwart Watson and I pray Gladstone appreciates what he has in you."

"You doubt the government's reason?" I asked.

"As if Britain, of all nations upon the earth, does not have the seamen for the job? Or that there are not a solid hundred thousand river-men in Cairo who could all be had for a few thousand pounds and upon a moment's notice? Come Watson."

At times my friend's tongue was as sharp as his intellect and no doubt he was right enough. If I were honest about it, Egypt likely had a million rivermen who could and would have done the job, and he was assuredly correct that they could have been got for a pittance at the snap of the fingers.

"No my friend," Holmes sighed, sadly, "I very much fear that Gordon Pasha, for all his nobility and courage, along with his faithful officers and brave men, and the tens of thousands of innocent civilians in Khartoum, are doomed to be sacrificed upon the altar of governmental impotence."[35]

I didn't want to believe that hope was already lost, but I contented myself instead with a book on the Middle East by Bayard Taylor, which I'd recently purchased at an excellent little shop on the High Street, a place called Chartiers."[36]

---

[35] Gordon Pasha, when he accepted the position of Governor-General of the Sudan, which at the time was, with Egypt, a satellite of the Ottoman Empire, he was given the honorary Ottoman title of Pasha. He was also to be known as Chinese Gordon, for his role in ending the Taiping Rebellion in China.

[36] The Lands of the Saracen or Pictures of Palestine, Asia Minor, etc., by Bayard Taylor, Pub. by Putnam, ©1856.

As the evening progressed I felt the sudden and strange sensation that I was being watched and looking up I found Holmes piercing eyes set upon me. It was quite unnerving actually and even more so for its rarity. He was holding a small piece of yellow parchment between his fingers.

"What is it?" I enquired.

He neither blinked nor spoke, but only gazed deeply at me.

"Holmes!" I called, "What is the paper?"

"I have…something to tell you," said he, handing it over.

The thing had some faded scribbles upon it and looked as if it had been in a gentleman's pocket for a good long time, even years perhaps. It was worn and the edges were the exposed fibers of the parchment.

"You'll require this," he said, quietly, as he handed me his magnifying glass.

"Hardly," I said, as I figured the first word upon the paper. "No, it's Hardy, then C-V?" I muttered, for it might just as easily have been an O-V. Then I decoded the last word, "Bannister."

I looked at my friend puzzled.

"I can make nothing of this mystification of words and letters," I said, "Hardy, C-V or O-V, and Bannister! What does it signify Holmes? A code?"

"It is C-V, if that helps at all Watson?"

"O-V or C-V, it's still a mystery to me."

"It is a memento," Holmes announced, simply.

"A memento? Like the ghastly human skin you showed me from the house on Granby Street?"

"Exactly so," said he.

"And where did you get this?"

"In the house on Granby Street, in a frame next to the one you just mentioned."

"Then this is tied to that devil Fyldene," I cried. "Why did you not give it to Inspector Redgrave or even Lestrade? And what does it mean?"

"It signifies crime my good man and I left a rough copy in its place. If the police can break it..."

"Another crime? And by Fyldene?" I said.

Holmes was deep in thought. That he'd taken the paper away with him from the crime scene puzzled me, but not as much as the fact that he'd not informed either of the Inspectors who were there. Some at Scotland Yard, Lestrade among them, had accused Holmes of toying with the law, as they put it. The reality was that my friend considered himself to be above the law. He saw it as a human invention and so, both flawed and relative to the time and place of its application or its idleness, whichever the powers that be at the time deemed most advantageous to their cause. He viewed himself thus a representative of justice, which in his view was universal, omnitemporal, and more or less unchanging.

"I must work with the law my good fellow," he once told me, "but make no mistake about it, it is justice I work for."

"This paper represents at least three crimes," said he, gravely.

"This little paper represents three crimes?" I stammered out. "Murders? Beyond the murders of the young women?"

"Yes and the first is identified by the word Hardy. The second is simply C-V and the last is Bannister."

"So not like the banister on a stairway?"

"No, you'll notice that the Bannister upon the paper is capitalized and has two 'n's' instead of one. This points to a name, not an architectural feature, and corresponds with the only other obvious name in the list, Hardy."

"And the C-V?"

"Well, taken with its proximity to two names, I should say that the letters are concerned with a hyphenated name which Fyldene recorded simply by its initials."

"That is certainly possible," I declared, looking at the paper again. When Holmes showed me the scrap of paper I hadn't thought of that possibility.

"C-V," he repeated.

"On the face of it you must admit, however, that it is very strange the man would write out two of the names in his list and then record the third as initials."

"Perhaps," my friend replied, "but surely the truly significant point is what name the C-V stands for, wouldn't you agree."

"There are the Cleverley-Vernet's, in Suffolk," I said, "like you're your French ancestor, Vernet. I was in school with one of the Cleverley-Vernet's you know?"

"Indeed," Holmes replied, unamused, ignoring my remark about his French ancestry.

"I suppose the only other name I know with those initials is the Colborn-Vessey's, in Kent."

"There is also the Cadmon-Vickers family in Liverpool Watson, the importers, but somehow I don't believe this refers to them."

"Then who? For between the two of us we've named every C-V in Britain have we not?"

"Not quite my good man."

"Then you'll have to tell me. I thought the names we'd already gotten were the limit."

"Fyldene was a diplomat. Can you not think of another like him who carried a C-V name?"

"Caldor-Vaughn," I exclaimed, amazed that I'd recalled it. "Sir Malcolm Caldor-Vaughn, he served as a diplomat in the Araby didn't he? It might have been around the same time Fyldene was there. But he left to run for Parliament."

"And he held his seat until his death..." Holmes said, with a significant pause.

"Which was in...June!"

"So can you recall who this Hardy might be?"

"I know Bannister," I cried. "Richard Bannister, Lord Carnwicke. The announcement of his death ran in the papers barely a month ago," I said.

"He was also in the Diplomatic Corp, although he began his career much earlier than Fyldene," Holmes remarked.

"And he had plum postings straight from the gate,"[37] I noted.

"Minister Plenipotentiary to the Sultan," my friend replied. "The youngest man ever to hold that post I believe they mentioned in the papers. The man must have had connections."

"And they carried him through his career."

"He ended up the British Ambassador to the French, in Paris," I added.

"He was there in '58 when Felice Orsini and his cutthroats attempted to assassinate the French Emperor and Empress,"[38] Holmes reminded,

"Maybe that was one of the reasons he was awarded those titles Mrs. Fyldene spoke about."

"And Edward Hardy was the third noteworthy British diplomat to die this year Watson. He had a successful career in India and helped put down the Mutiny. Then he became Britain's chief agent in Ottoman Arabia and Mesopotamia, stationed at Bagdad in fact, where he was Fyldene's superior. He died in May, a month before Caldor-Vaughn."

---

[37] Plum Posting – a desirable position or job.
[38] Felice Orsini was an Italian revolutionary who with a small group of accomplices attempted to assassinate French Emperor Napoleon III with three bombs. The Emperor and his wife were unhurt but eight were killed and one-hundred-and-forty were wounded.

"So this faded list," I said, realizing only then its full import, "is a list of men Fyldene had issues with...and you think he killed them," I exclaimed, "based upon the fact that they all died this year?"

"But it is a significant fact Watson, as is the fact that they all worked with Henry Fyldene. It is beyond the limit of human ingenuity to furnish an explanation which would cover both these facts, but I offer a third, which must remove all doubt."

"If all three fit into this scheme, then, as you've said before, a hypothesis may become a solution. So what is your third outstanding fact?"

"The very fact that the paper you now hold was found in a frame hanging upon the wall of Henry Fyldene's secret office. Next to the framed tattoo of the delicate wrist of the woman named Tereza Amalia Rosenberg no less. This removes all doubt that the three dead diplomats were murdered. That paper, like the framed tattoo, was Fyldene's macabre memento to his revenge and...as such it is proof of his crime."

"But how did they die?" I insisted, for murder had not been the cause in any of the deaths.

Holmes leaned back in his chair with half-closed eyes. "You must admit that the idea that all of this is merely a coincidence is an impossibility. Fyldene had more grim murders afoot than we at first suspected. These dead diplomats are a sequel to his earlier murders. It might even be argued that he saw the deaths of those young, unmarried, virgin women, as a holy sacrifice in preparation for his magnum opus."[39]

I stared at Holmes, horrified and silent.

"What you have just described is something out of the bowels of hell," I remarked. "It could only come from a mind..." I stopped speaking as I had no words to convey my disgust.

---

[39] magnum opus – Latin for "great work", also, masterpiece.

"Let us admit that there something unnatural and even unholy about the strange and sudden fall of Henry Fyldene," he said.

"That will not be hard to do," I confessed.

"Fyldene's *madness* appears to have stemmed from the revelation of his wife's infidelity and the boy's true paternity, but this is an illusion. Though those things were the stimuli which drove his actions in '73, there was something else which predated them, which had prepared the ground."

"His disappointment over his career must be seen to have some place in all that," I hazarded.

"Right you are Watson, right you are. When his retirement brought him back to London, where the very men he considered his chief tormentors were all collected, his plan was set in stone."

"But why return to the killing of more young women after so long a time, if these three men were his true targets?"

"Ah, there you've said it my friend. If the men were indeed his *true targets*…then the murders of the young women would merely have been…"

"A distraction to the police, to all of London in fact," I barely whispered. "The return of the mad killer of young women would prove a sensation."

"Indeed Watson and it has served Fyldene well. Don't be shocked when I tell you that I believe Fyldene had foreseen all of this when, in '73, he began with the first murder of a poor immigrant woman. Consider how worn that paper is."

"You mean that even then he was preparing for the murder of his enemies and that this list was..."

"Amazing isn't it? A mediocre diplomat at best, lacking intellect and motivation, yet proved a master murderer possessed of vision and control. As I've said before though my good fellow, evil awakens a malignant genius and gives birth to a great many malicious deeds. I believe that Fyldene began his planning the very day he discovered he'd been cuckolded by his beautiful wife."

"Nothing can justify his actions," I affirmed, "but the shock of that betrayal, and that the fact was so obvious to all of his peers and friends, that would have been truly maddening."

"Yes it would and it goes a long way to justify young Mr. Broughton's harsh view of marriage, does it not?" Holmes offered.

"It is but one example in millions, however," I replied, defensively.

"But now, what did Fyldene want with these young women? What did they really supply him?"

"The distraction surely, as we've already said, although it galls me to think of those innocent women being sacrificed for so terrible a cause."

"There was nothing winning in the man, but his experience had shown him the *vulnerability* of those women. It was their very helplessness which drew him to target them. That is what they truly offered Henry Fyldene, the Elder."

"And the sensational murders of those young women meant that no one would be focused on the random deaths of three elderly men, each with their own ailments no doubt. But you've not explained how he killed them or how he masked their murders so as to avoid detection."

"As to his means of murder Watson, I only have theories at this time, and I will not prejudice my mind or yours by repeating them. If you are up for a midnight journey though, I propose we put my theories to the test."

"Whatever you need," said I, eagerly, for my friend had found me out years earlier.

The truth was that I shared Sherlock Holmes' love of all that was bizarre, outré, and outside the dull routine.[40] My experience had exposed me to the rush and pull of danger.

"Excellent my good fellow, but now to answer your question as to how Fyldene hid the murders of the three diplomats."

"Yes for no one but you, as far as I can tell, has understood that their deaths were in fact cold-blooded murders."

"He did nothing Watson. As things turned out he didn't have to do a thing. He left it all to that principle which you have already forwarded and described so clearly."

"Which would that be?" I asked.

---

[40] Outré – shocking, unconventional.

"All that was required to cover the murders of the three was that each was *elderly*, and being from the monied class, they would not have lacked for doctors to focus upon their ailments."

"So one was put down to pleurisy, one to a heart attack, and the other, to what?"

"The gall bladder."

"The gall bladder?" I repeated, shaking my head in disbelief. "And that was all he needed?"

"That is how I read the matter."

"I see, and Fyldene knew as much?"

"Exactly, he was from their class and realized that both family and police often accepted the quiet death of an elderly relative without either question or suspicion. All that was required was that they be elderly. Beyond that he believed the method he'd chosen for their murders would raise no unnecessary attention and would, therefore, go completely undetected."

"But you won't tell me what that method was?"

"Poison my good fellow," said he, "but as I said, that is only a theory at this point and we must confirm it before we can be satisfied."

"And that is what you need my help for?"

"I enlisted Lestrade earlier, as he seems of all of them to have the least upon his plate at present. He wired earlier that he'd gotten permission from the Bannisters and the Hardy's to search the dead men's rooms. He'll stop by in the morning with his findings."

"And does he know your reason for his labors or have you kept him in the dark?"

"He is doing me a favor, doubtlessly in the hope that the next tip I give will not go to Inspector Redgrave. I have to admit though that there may well be no good purpose served by the public disclosure as to the true cause of their deaths."

"So, with the killer dead, this is in some ways an academic exercise."

"The killer is dead, that much is true enough, but there may still be reason enough to pursue it."

"And the Caldor-Vaughns?"

"That one falls to us my friend, as the family has retreated to the country to grieve and has not responded to the Inspector's inquiries."

"So we'll be breaking in?" I said, little surprised.

It was clear that being a consulting detective had definite advantages over the official forces, but there were times I felt Holmes took liberties.

"We will suppose, for argument's sake, that the family's townhouse, Laughton Hall, has been left in the care of a small detachment of servants under the lead of a second footman," said he.

"Or even the third footman," I offered.

"I suppose even that is possible."

"Which is better than having a full household with all hands-upon-deck," I remarked.

"But we must hope that the Irregulars arrive with our information on Capshaw soon."

"Yes," I said, "so we may get to our burgling."

"Burgling implies theft Watson," said he.

"And you don't intend to take anything away with you?"

In all our former adventures of the type, there was only one which I could recall in which we'd left empty handed and that had resulted in a crime of another kind.

"We will say that by one o'clock the household will be fast asleep. By some careful lock work it is quite possible we will wake no one. In any case it is likely that when they rise in the morning they will have no idea we were even there."

"With Laughton Hall only a short drive away we may return no later than two in the morning."

"If we are successful my good fellow, then you will be guaranteed several hours of sleep before we have to leave for whatever location the Irregulars supply us."

My friend's ability to function without sleep was an established fact, but I was, alas, a mere mortal.

J. B. Varney

Chapter 9 – The Hour Grows Late

"The hour grows late Watson and yet no word arrives. I begin to fear that I asked too much."

"Come now," I reasoned, marking my page and closing my book, "if their past record is anything to go on, then even a mastiff could not hold more firmly to his prey than your Irregulars."

"It is kind of you to say so," said he, with a weak smile, "but I know for a fact that little Billy set you against them from the start."

Little Billy, or rather, William Wiggins, was now a lean and lanky thirteen-year-old. Upon our first meeting, to which Holmes had just referred, this chap had pinched my grandfather's gold pocket watch. I'd gotten it back, but at the cost of what the boys called, "a small donation."

"Just because they robbed and fleeced me," I said, "it doesn't hold that I'd refuse to recognize their special...*gifts*."

"That's the spirit my good fellow and perhaps you're right. I'll just stretch my legs a bit and give them a few more minutes.

Not quite thirty minutes later the ring of the bell, which my friend had so long awaited, finally came and two boys were shown in, cap in hand. They half bowed to Sherlock Holmes.

"Sorry to disturb ye at this hour Mr. 'Olmes."

"If it is to bring me good news boys," said he, "then rest assured all shall be forgiven."

"T'is indeed Mr. 'Olmes but with expenses it comes dear."

"Never mind that," my friend said, reassuringly. "I will see you set to rights if the information is of quality, as always."

"We took turns trailing the man as he seemed skittish, if ye kin."[41]

"I follow," Holmes replied, encouragingly.

"Well 'ee took the Edgeware Train, ta' Great Northern, and got off at Mill Hill, the East Station."

This Edgeware the lads had spoken of was a modest village ten miles north and a little west of London City and Mill Hill was a stop or two before that. It was still rural country with a few well-known manors and estates scattered around even fewer villages. The one estate that I remembered at the moment was that of the great reformer against slavery, William Wilberforce, at High Hill.[42]

"'Ee walked a little way up Ridgeway Road Mr. 'Olmes," the other boy added, wanting to do his part no doubt.

"A small place Sir with a placard out front what reads Woodvale, just beyond the junction with Holders Hill Road, on the left."

"And he remains there?" Holmes asked.

"Unlocked the door and went in."

"We minded 'im for an 'our but 'ee stayed put."

---

[41] "Kin" or sometimes "ken", archaic for "understand."
[42] Abolition of the transatlantic slave trade was achieved in Parliament in 1807.

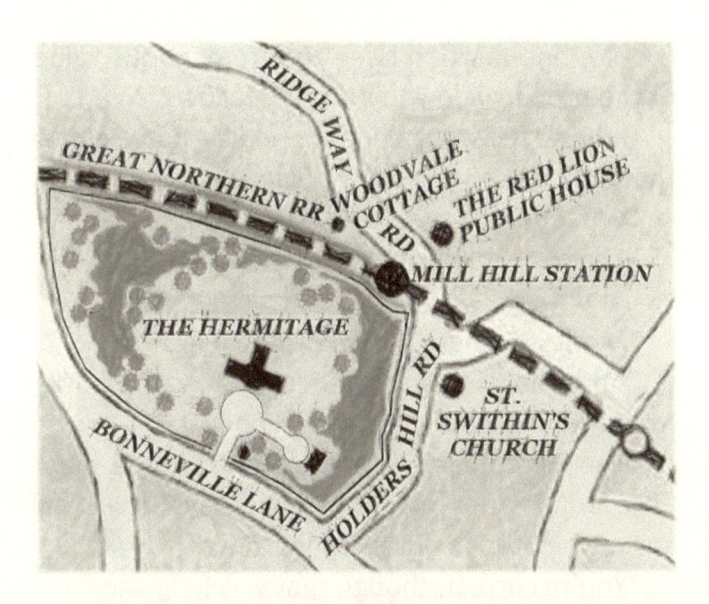

"You all did admirably boys," Holmes said, "and I trust that two extra sovereigns would cover all the extra expenses?"

"Oy, that 'ould be grand Mr. 'Olmes, grand!"

"And you will see to the set distribution?"

"Rules is rules Mr. 'Olmes. We all knows that."

After the boys left, Holmes took down a bundle of maps and scattered them recklessly about the table until his eyes lit upon the one he wanted.

"Look here Watson," said he, excited. "Mill Hill, there, see, the East Station, and Ridgeway Road, and there, Holders Hill Road.

"That means Freddy Capshaw's cottage is right there," I said, pointing. "It backs up right on the Great Northern's rail track," I observed. "That can't be pleasant with all the noise."

"No, but you don't see the tremendous value of the property do you my good fellow?"

Holmes' was speaking in riddles now, either that or I'd miss something obvious.

"What do you see there?" he asked.

"That was Wilberforce's estate, High Hill."

"And there?"

"Morley Grange," I read off the map.

"And what is this, located just across the tracks from Mr. Capshaw's cottage, Woodvale?"

"The Hermitage," I read aloud from the map. "The print is tiny but I believe it says it was an ancient residence of the Bonneville's."

"You're correct, though that was long ago."

"So now the place is for let?" I asked.

"The number of large houses close in around Woodvale is obviously limited," said he, gesturing across the map, "and I have little doubt the agents would verify that the Hermitage was recently let."

"And with Mr. Frederick Capshaw here," I said, pointing to the location of the cottage upon the map, "you believe the key to this whole tangled skein of a mystery lies at the Hermitage."

"On the face of it the disappearance of Henry Fyldene did not promise to be a very complex case, not at first. He would turn up soon enough, or his body would, the result of an unfortunate accident or foul play, and we'd never be required. Once Mrs. Fyldene got us involved and we learned the unique factors involved in the mystery, well."

"Yes," I said, comprehending his point.

"The connection to the Torso Murders and the discovery of the dead diplomats, that presented us with some remarkable novelties. I've said there is nothing new under the sun, nothing which has not been done before, but this case Watson, taken as a whole, is a rare exception to that rule."

"But I thought you didn't like exceptions to your rules," I replied, having heard this as well.

"I don't," said he, confirming his principle, "and that should demonstrate what an extraordinary case we are now involved in."

"So we're off to burgle Laughton Hall shortly and, if we are not locked up or shot, then it will be the Great Northern to Edgeware in the morning?"

"Yes," Holmes affirmed, "we'll see Lestrade in the morning and then set off for Mill Hill, the East Station upon the Ridgeway Road."

"I'll pack for an extended stay then."

"An excellent notion Watson, for Mrs. Fyldene has retained our services and ordered we spare no expense and no pains to return her son to her. If you're ready in an hour it will be sufficient. The game will soon be afoot again."

With that my friend turned to the window and the lamplit Baker Street below.

An hour later I emerged from my room.

"You are ready?" he asked,

"As I will ever be," I smiled.

"Then you'll want this," he said, handing me a strip of black silk. I recognized the mask which would cover a good portion of my face and slid it into my pocket. We'd used them before.

We ventured out onto a silent Baker Street just as the fog arrived to hush the few sounds of the night thereabouts, and cast their large, golden halos around every streetlamp.

"We'll have to go to Marylebone to catch a cab," I remarked, as we turned left and started south along our street. The only sound the tapping of our canes.

"Laughton Hall has a ground floor side door for the servants and opens to the servants' stairwell and a delivery hallway," Holmes said, as we walked along.[43] "It is this door by which we'll gain our entrance. You'll take the stairwell to Sir Malcolm's private rooms above, while I take the ground floor hall to his private study. I've been assured the Caldor-Vaughn's left promptly in the wake of Sir Malcolm's death, so you should find the place undisturbed."

"And what is it I'm looking for," I asked.

"Anything edible. Toffee, a brittle, lemon or peppermint sweets, you know the sort of thing. Pomfret cakes or even a Kendal is possible."[44]

---

[43] In Victorian Britain "the ground floor" was what Americans called "the first floor." The "first floor" was the "second floor."
[44] Pomfret cakes, originally Pontefract cakes, are a black, coin-sized sweet of licorice. Kendal Mint Cake is a peppermint

"However," he continued, "if it hasn't yet been cleared away, I very much expect it to be one of those exclusive treats in a beautiful little tin or box with the elaborate labels. The kind with just a few treats, a half-dozen or so, to represent a rare delicacy of great value and promote consumption while discouraging sharing. It would have been important to Fyldene that his victims eat every treat at one sitting if possible. Perhaps some of the French-styled soft-center candies, from Paris of course. Turkish Delight from one of the finest makers, that is always a possibility, or the prestige chocolates from Belgium or Switzerland to be sure, and again in a glorious tin."

"I suppose one of the bitter chocolates would have covered the taste of most poisons better than anything else."

"An excellent observation," said he, "and I'd be surprised if we don't find that Fyldene used just such a vehicle for his murders."

"Then what is your hypothesis?" I asked. "That the killer simply sent his tainted treats through the post, hoping that they would come to his intended targets and that they wouldn't be shared with others?"

"We realized that Fyldene had initiated contact with the unfortunate immigrant women who then came to England, so they expected to find him."

---

flavored sugary confection which, according to legend, comes from Kendal in Cumbria, England.

"Yes, it spared him the need to persuade them to trust a stranger."

"I propose he used a similar technique here."

"With the treats?" I asked.

"Precisely. What if, instead of receiving a tin of delicacies from a total stranger, Messrs. Hardy, Bannister, and Caldor-Vaughn, had a card from an old and trusted friend accompanying the gift, what would they think?"

"But might not they contact their friends and thereby discover the deception which had been played upon them?"

"It is not likely and, if he feared such a risk he could easily choose someone who would be difficult to reach. After all Fyldene had worked with these men. He knew who they knew in India and in the Ottoman regions of Mesopotamia and Araby. There are any number of stratagems he might have used without concern of discovery, such was the beauty of his plan."

"It was diabolical!" I exclaimed, as we reached Marylebone Road, picked up a Hansom, and gave the address in Hampstead.

"You used the past tense," Holmes remarked, once we were upon our way.

"What's that?"

"I said you used the past tense Watson."

"Yes. Fyldene is dead after all."

Holmes was silent and the only sound in the dark night was the clip-clop of our horse's hooves echoing off the cobbles.

"So with Fyldene dead," said he, "you hold that he cannot do further evil?"

Holmes' point stunned me.

"You said that an investigation into the dead diplomats was merely an academic exercise," he reminded, "yet, if..."

"If another tin of treats is even now in the post, speeding its way to a fourth diplomat..."

"Or several tins," said he, gravely, "to several former associates, what then?"

"Death, death!" I cried. "This devil can still kill," I exclaimed, "even from his grave!"

"Yes my friend, even from the grave."

"But wait Holmes, for the paper he framed only held three names! So it holds there are no more."

"That was why I gave you the magnifying glass Watson," said he, mysteriously. "So that you'd see the lines below those three names."

"Surely those where merely scratches with the lead and not actual names!"

"I'm afraid Watson, that we must consider the possibility that Mr. Henry Fyldene commissioned another party to see to the distribution of the cards and the poisoned tins. He only needed to see to the poisoning of the treats themselves, then hand everything over."

"There could as easily be thirty tins as three then," I groaned, feeling sick with shock. "The third party would follow his instructions and send everything out upon the set dates to the list of men Fyldene had provided. If this is true Holmes, there is no way to stop it."

"So you see Watson, although the devil is dead, this is anything but an academic exercise."

"This is nightmarish Holmes, but is possible?"

"Completely possible I'm sorry to say and in the absence of knowing, we must proceed as if it is a reality."

"What can we do?"

"I've sent a message to the Home Office earlier in the day."

"But what can they do?"

"They can notify every man who ever worked with Henry Fyldene, the Elder, and warn them, although that admittedly will take a good deal of time. Meanwhile tomorrow's papers will correct the murderer's name to Fyldene and will alert all those who might stand to be in danger. It will also insure that the person Fyldene brought in to carry out his plan knows too."

"So that will expose Fyldene and warn those who worked with him at the same time.

"Indeed Watson, although I feel for his family for there are none more innocent, but it cannot be helped."

Few people understood Holmes' humanity as I did. I, however, guilty of focusing upon the more sensational aspects of our adventures, as Holmes had once accused, had not shown that side of my friend as well or as often as I might have done.

"You see Watson, while thirty-three Granby Street was rife with evidence regarding the killings of the young women, I don't believe it was an accident there was no evidence at all regarding the dead diplomats. No files, documents, tins, cards, or plans, only the cryptic scrap of paper marked with Hardy, C-V, and Bannister and displayed for his satisfaction alone."

"He never dreamed there was someone alive who could comprehend the meaning of that faded scrap of parchment."

"It was a complete and unintelligible cypher," Holmes confirmed. "He wanted the police to see only the women. They truly were the sacrifices he'd offered the world, all in order to hide his true targets of his bounding revenge."

"And had you not exposed him he might have gotten away with everything, as it is..."

"Yes, quite, but here we are my friend, a block or so from Laughton Hall."

Here we paid off our cab and pulled our coats close for the cold. Once we reached the large, dark block of the residence we put our masks on. It was a remarkable how simple it was to transform two gentlemen into London criminals and felons.

Holmes rolled his kit out and the door opened in less than a minute. We were greeted by the reassuring warmth and stillness of Laughton Hall.

"Good luck Watson," he whispered as he crept away, vanishing down the hall.

Our plan was to meet outside the back door in fifteen minutes. As a contingency plan in case we were discovered, however, we were to make our escape as best we could and rejoin each other back at 221B.

I lit one of the candle stubs we brought for the purpose and made my way slowly up the narrow, winding servant's stair to the first floor as best I could. The house was such an inky blackness that even so little a flame cast a great light, throwing haunting shadows all around me.

Once or twice I was so taken by a sudden black shadow jumping silently nearby, the work of the flickering flame of my candle, that I thought I'd have a seizure. These first feelings of fear passed away though and I soon found myself exhilarated by the danger, with every nerve on edge.

My pocket watch revealed that I'd already used a third of my allotted time and I began to rush from room to room. Finally I found a room which, for its size and grandeur couldn't be mistaken for any but the master's suite. The giant balusters at each corner of the bed supported a heavy top, red velvet curtains and a carved headboard which could've come down from the time of Henry VIII.

Henry Fyldene

I nearly knocked a vase over at one point and only by the greatest effort did I manage to catch it before it shattered in a great crash.

I thought of my friend searching the downstairs with his usual calm, deliberate method and knew the odds favored him finding the clue or clues.

Then in one corner I spied one of the high desks with a flat top for storage and the slanted surface that worked as both the desktop as well as the lid to a large storage area beneath. It was of the kind used by engineers and accountants. Against the wall on the flat portion of the desk was a fine golden inkwell, expensive pens, pencils, and an varied assortment of other items, dim in the candlelight.

I leaned upon the desk for a moment and began sorting through a stack of the papers and packages, when I suddenly heard the creak of the floor somewhere behind me and close at hand.

I didn't dare turn and look. I'd already made my decision of what to do in such a case and I knew that the only safety lay in legging it. As I spun I could see a flash of lantern light coming through the open door, its shining patch spreading quickly in my direction. I didn't know if the man was armed or not but I reasoned that if he were, I stood a better chance of him missing me if I was on the move, so I redoubled my effort. Whether he was the second footman or the third was unimportant to me as I raced off.

I got back to Baker Street as best I could and waited nervously for nearly two hours before Holmes finally returned.

"It got noticeably hot back there once you'd set off the footman Watson, and when the police arrived, well…"

"And how you escaped their dragnet?"

"Well, I had the good fortune of finding a little used stairwell which opened off Sir Malcolm's study," said he, glibly, "and no one looked. Still, it looks like it was all for naught as we came away empty handed."

"Speak for yourself," I said, setting a gleaming, golden tin down upon the table in front of him.

"Chocolat Noir," he read, "Amédée Kohler & Fils in Lausanne Suisse."

My French was not equal to Holmes, but it was adequate to this challenge at least.

Amadeus Kohler & Sons Lausanne Switzerland, Dark Chocolate, was the translation.

"You did it Watson," said he, clearly relieved.

"Yes but I found no card or letter accompanying the tin, though I looked through everything on the top of the desk."

"But it is enough to either support or disprove my theory in the morning, when we see Lestrade," he said, soberly. "Very well done my friend."

J. B. Varney

Chapter 10 – The Hermitage

"You appear to have been very prompt with your packing," said he, the following morning at the breakfast table. My bags were all lined up at the door."

"I'm bringing my slouch hat and my Homburg. And you?" I asked, for I saw only his carpet bag.

"I'll take just the one bag and support the local tradesmen in the borough of Barnet, as my needs require."[45]

"And you've told Mrs. Hudson?"

"She declared herself pleased to have a chance at some peace and quiet for once."

The poor woman was the soul of tolerance and, had she but been of the Catholic persuasion, she would most definitely have been sainted.

"Is there any other news?" I asked, seeing he had a folded copy of The Times beside him.

"Merely the celebratory ripples coming from the closing of the Torso Murders, the Tottenham Court Road business and all that," said he. "It seems they cannot say enough, now that the true killer has been identified."

"So would I be right to think that Mr. Martin Hillblom has received clemency," I laughed as I looked over his shoulder at the print.

---

[45] Modern Edgeware lies in the Boroughs of Barnet , Harrow, and Brent.

My laughter caught in my throat when I saw the name Fyldene writ large across the page and recalled Holmes' sadness of the previous day.

"So the Fyldene's will be in for it now."

"It is a tragic reality," said he.

"As young Henry is not in actual fact a Fyldene he will be free of that name soon enough, I suppose."

"He might take his father's name," Holmes offered, "although Mrs. Fyldene has provided us only his father's first name. Still it is more than enough to assure us upon the point at least."

"What then would he call himself?" I asked.

"I would recommend the application of Ibn-Abdul. Although I cannot boast in my Arabic, it is at least enough to be sure of the accuracy of that name."

Ibn-Abdul was literally *son of Abdul* so Holmes was correct that it was accurate, but the entire exercise had left me a little perplexed. If we could find the young man alive, would he in fact disdain the name he'd carried his entire life?

It was at that moment there came Lestrade's pull upon the bell and soon we heard his quick step upon the stair.

"Good morning Inspector," Holmes said. "Hot tea on a cold morning?"

"I don't mind if I do Mr. Holmes. We were out upon your assignment a good bit of yesterday I don't mind telling you."

"I need not tell you how much your help is appreciated Lestrade," said he, as he delivered the tea.

"I suppose not Mr. Holmes, but that isn't the same as telling us why we just troubled those two grieving families the way we did. It was terrible."

"Now Inspector," my friend replied, "you know better than most that sometimes saying nothing to the family is the kindest thing one can do. I have no doubt that they would agree in this case, so I must keep our secret for now. Perhaps someday you'll be able to read of my reason for doing so in one of Dr. Watson's stories."

This didn't satisfy the Inspector overly much, but there was little to be done about it so he accepted Holmes' explanation.

"We looked for the items you described," said he, "and this is what we found in the townhouse of Sir Richard Bannister."

He emptied one pocket, producing an identical tin to the one I'd gotten at Laughton Hall. Then he laid down an embossed greeting card. Holmes' eyes flashed with excitement but he controlled himself and kept his seat.

"And Sir Edward Hardy?" He asked.

"Another tin," Lestrade said, "but no card or letter to go along with it, despite our hours of searching. I know there's some great significance here," he said, gesturing to the items, "but for the life of me I can't put it together Mr. Holmes."

"Well you've been quite helpful Inspector and if there is anything else I'll be sure to let you know. In the meantime you and your men have my sincere appreciation. If there is anything I can put your way in the future, rest assured I will do so."

"That's something then," said he, unhappily. Then gulping the last of his tea the poor man, who'd been robbed of his glory in the Tottenham Court Road Mystery, rose and took his leave.

"You really should have given him something Holmes," I said, sympathetically.

"I dared not Watson, not without giving all the game away. As it was I can't imagine how he didn't put the pieces together."

"And would that have been so bad?"

"If exposing the deaths of the three diplomats as murders only hurts the grieving families more, brings them unwanted attention, and keeps their names in front of the public even longer, all while the killer of their loved ones is already dead and buried, I couldn't justify it. Depending on how the Home Office handles the matter, someone may yet figure out the mystery, but between ourselves Watson, I'd rather not aid in that outcome."

"Well you have all the evidence now," I noted, looking at the tins and the card, "and without that I don't know how anyone else could solve it."

Holmes took up the embossed card with the silver letter "R" from the little table and examined it minutely for several minutes.

"Listen to this my good fellow, then tell me your thoughts," he said. "Fyldene starts out by referring to Sir Richard Bannister as 'Dickie,' thereby putting their relationship upon familiar terms from the outset."

"A cunning devil," said I.

"Very true and because he knew these men so well he knew just who to mention to make their connection seem a genuine one. He speaks here of Pemberton and Grimsby as if they were mutual friends. 'We were reminiscing about the old days and I determined to send you a little box of my favorite chocolates by way of a reminder from your old friends still in Bagdad.'"

"What does he sign it?" I asked.

"There's the marvel," Holmes said, admiringly. "In keeping with an old friend he simply scribbles out his name. Certainly Bannister would have known who 'R' was and perhaps the signature is an accurate one, as Fyldene's wicked genius could have spurred him to copy it all those years ago in Araby. Either way, Pemberton, Grimsby, and the unintelligible 'R,' were doubtlessly true friends of the late Sir Richard Bannister, Lord Carnwicke."

"I am struck by one thing Holmes," I confessed.

"And what is that my good fellow?"

"That if Henry Fyldene, the Elder, had applied just half the attention and energy to his career that he did to his revenge, he might easily have excelled them all."

"Ah Watson, you've discovered the great truth upholding the establishment of criminality. If the practitioners of *the ignoble arts* were willing to give an honest vocation just half the attention and energy which they give to their endless schemes and crimes, they would have most assuredly been notable successes indeed. Very likely they would also have been the stalwarts, rather than the banes of their respective communities."

Holmes had often referred to the vocation of crime, for those who'd made it a life's calling, as *the ignoble arts*. There were certainly few among the law abiding who understood the risks and sacrifices the criminal was willing to take as well as did Mr. Sherlock Holmes. He would point out that the felon not only gambles with his own life and happiness, but with the lives and happiness of his victims and those who are dependent upon him as well. I'd known little of that dark world prior to meeting him, but the last years together had been a thorough introduction.

"I must admit that even I can now see a strange genius in Fyldene, having seen his orchestration of his revenge," said I.

We took the Great Northern north and arrived at Mill Hill Station in the chilly midmorning. The silver lace of the frost still clung wherever the shadows fell. We took rooms at the nearby public house which went by the ubiquitous name of "The Red Lion."

"Doubtless as a reference to your family crest Holmes," I remarked, once we reached our rooms, for such was the Holmes' crest.

He had that singular expression he always had when he was considering something dangerous.

"Indubitably," said he, unamused. "How do you feel about a brisk walk in the open-air Watson?"

"You have a plan then?" I asked.

"I do," said he, pulling the lace curtain back and looking down upon the humble thoroughfare of Ridgeway Road, "and as we are here to investigate the Hermitage and not Capshaw's cottage, one of us must see what awaits us at the main gate."

"Then I suppose you'll go by way of the cottage, across the tracks, and over the stone wall at the rear of the property."

"The verge is especially thick just there," said he, "and with your sudden appearance in front of the old Manor House, the distraction should be adequate to insure I go unnoticed."

"And what is to be my line?"

"You can use the age and connections of the place as a cover for yourself, perhaps inquire about tours of the historic old Bonneville Manor? Your great aunt was a servant there or something of that nature. You know the routine."

I did know the routine, having used it before.

"The solution to this mystery lies just there my good fellow," he said, pointing through the trees and across at the towers of the ancient estate.

"If Mrs. Fyldene's son is still alive we'll find him there, I'm sure of it."

"And if he is not Holmes, what then?"

"If the young man is dead Watson, we will find the place empty and doubtlessly in a shambles from the sudden flight of the inhabitants."

"But how would they know?"

"Capshaw is their man my good fellow! Have you forgotten? And the Irregulars tracked him here. He wouldn't have lost a single moment informing his employers that Dr. John Watson and Mr. Sherlock Holmes were hot upon their trail."

"Of course," I said, "but why would Capshaw betray his friend?"

"Recall that up until a few weeks ago the two young men had never met. Capshaw was sought out and paid to do a job for them. His shared *commonalities* with the young Henry were no doubt the great and obvious selling points for his employer. With the purchase of a membership at the Oxford & Cambridge Club and the acquisition of a wardrobe capable of passing him off as a true member of the class, Capshaw was thrust into young Henry's way. Thus their plan was enacted and, in time, their man made his approach."

"And he went voluntarily, young Henry I mean? Is that our working hypothesis?"

"He went Watson and the very way he went can only tend to highlight the fact that the young man felt no overwhelming reason to resist."

"Well then I'll put my gaiters and cape-coat on, grab my Blackthorn walking stick, and go pass myself off as a back country squire upon holiday."

"Good man," said he, "and if you find anything remarkable you can inform me when we meet back here. Perhaps later, after we've formulated our next move, you would care to join me in the dining room for a supper of the establishment's famous roast beef."

"I am entirely at your service," I said, with a tap on the brim of my Homburg.[46]

With that I took my leave of Sherlock Holmes and ventured out into the countryside of Barnet. The day had warmed and the frost was nearly all gone from the roadside bushes and brambles. I strolled leisurely down Holders Hill Road enjoying the sunshine and trying to *inhabit* the role of a vacationing amateur historian, soon to call upon the good folk at the Hermitage in hope of a tour.

Holmes had often said that the key to his disguises was his ability to *inhabit the role*. He believed himself to be the person he was set upon modeling to the world. "Be the hostler!" he said.[47]

I was not sure how good I might be at such a task, but if there were ever a role which was naturally suited to me, then it was the one my friend had now assigned me.

---

[46] Homburg Hat – soft felt gentleman's hat.
[47] Hostler – stable worker, groom.

I'd long been interested in history and as an amateur I had no need to impress anyone with the instant recall of archaic facts and information.

With the soft sun shining upon my face and the high stone wall separating the ancient estate of the Bonneville's estate from Holders Hill Road working as a windbreak for me, the day seemed natural for a stroll about the countryside.

I walked past an old stone church which looked to have medieval origins about its chancel.[48]

I realized there was no hurry and so stopped and turned to admire it.

"St. Swithin's Church," I read aloud off the sign.

This was the Saint for whom St. Swithin's Day, July 15th, had been named and as I recalled it he'd been an eighth century Church Deacon or the like. He lived in Worchester if I was correct.[49]

I leaned upon my Blackthorn walking stick and quoted something from memory which I had not thought of since my youth.

"On St. Swithin's Day if it dost rain, for forty days it shall remain."

"You remember the old rhymes," a quiet voice from behind me spoke, surprising me.

Turning I found a diminutive woman wrapped in a hand-spun shawl and kerchief, in the process of passing down the road on the far side.

---

[48] Chancel – area around the altar.
[49] St. Swithin, sometimes Swithun, a ninth-century Bishop of Winchester who humbly asked to be buried in a common grave.

"I do," I said, "but I'm afraid there are not many left with whom I can share the memory."

"I recollect them she said," flashing me a pretty smile, "and I say St. Swithin's rhyme as I pass 'ere, for good fortune."

"Then you pass the church every day?"

"Twice a day I do Sir," said she, "upon my way to work and then home again I do, and each time I remember the Saint's rhyme I do."

"I believe the old saying comes from the fact that they were going to tear the church down where Swithin was buried," I said.

"And it rained ever so hard and long too, so they gave up their wicked plan. They'd promised 'ta Saint that nothing would change ye see. But what brings ye to St. Swithin's?" she pried, gently.

"I'm an historian," I replied.

"Oh how grand," she cried, happily, giving me her best curtsy as if I was some great nob.[50] "Are ye from one of the Universities? Are you famous? Oh, I must remember your name Sir."

"No, no," I assured her, "I'm afraid I'm only a humble amateur, but I've come to tour the old manor house of the Bonneville Family."

"Oh dear, Sir," said she, the sadness and worry clear in her voice, "you've not heard then?"

"Heard what?" I replied, honestly concerned.

"The place 'as been let to band o' heathen Sir!"

---

[50] Nob, the archaic English term for a noble or notable person.

The woman was almost beside herself with fear and could barely look at me now.

"They are fierce Sir, that they are, and not a word of the English among 'em. Foreigners to the last man if I'm right."

"And how come you to know so much?"

"I am their biddy char Sir.[51] I keeps the place clean, although they don't make much fuss on that score, but I fear they won't look kindly upon you, a visitor and a famous gentleman, and so English to boot."

"What a pity and I've come all this way and even taken rooms at the Red Lion," said I. "I must at least ask I suppose. There could be no harm in asking could there?" I said, innocently.

"I shall pray for ye then, for ye seem a kindly sort, and 'andsome too," she replied, blushing, and then she took to her heels as if she were afraid to even be seen with me.

She'd said everything but that she'd mourn my passing, but as I watched her attractive form disappear around a bend in the estate's high wall, I wondered if her fears might be based upon something more concrete than mere hysteria.

I took a last look at St. Swithin's Church and turned and followed my anonymous informer at a relaxed pace set to see me before the Hermitage's gate in fifteen or twenty minutes.

---

[51] Biddy Char, Charlady, Charwoman, or sometimes simply "Char", the archaic English term for housecleaner.

Holmes had acquainted me with the map and by the time I turned right onto Bonneville Lane there was no trace of the little biddy char lady anywhere. She had put a good foot under her and made the main gate before I'd even turned the corner. It was an impressive feat.

I rang the bell at the old gatehouse but received no answer. After standing deep in thought for a while, and as the wrought iron gates stood wide open, I reasoned the new inhabitants expected their would-be visitors to announce themselves at the manor itself.

It was a pleasant walk up the graveled lane and the fine old park stretched away through oaks and maples, leafless for the coming winter, but still grand and stately.

Upon crossing the carriage circle I approached the heavy extension of a Gothic portico which offered its substantial shelter to the front door.

As I turned in, however, I was confronted by the oddest vision one would ever expect to find at an English country home and even though the charlady had warned me, I was stunned. There before me stood a dark man with a grim look, full-length black robe with golden trim, belting, and straps, a full Arabian headdress and a gleaming silver, curve-bladed sword of the type known as a Saracen.[52]

---

[52] The headdress is known as a keffiyeh and is held in place by bands or cords called an agal.

We stood there looking at each other for a long moment and I slowly realized that I must appear almost as odd to him as he did to me.

"Aas-salaam alaikum," I said, using almost my entire vocabulary of Arabic in a single go.[53]

---

[53] A traditional greeting meaning, "peace to you."

It was now my counterpart's turn to be amazed and I viewed his startled expression with some satisfaction.

"Wa 'alaykumu s-salām," he replied.

Then to my added surprise he stepped aside graciously, half-bowed to me in a friendly manner, and swung the great door open.

"You must be...the doctor?" a thin, small man in a red fez said in a clipped English accent.[54]

He stared down at me from the stairs, both hands buried deep in his pockets and his stark, black moustache bristling with suspicion.

"I am Dr. Watson."

"It matters not," he snapped, waving his hand.

"You will show this...man to the library and keep him there under guard until I command you otherwise," he said to a similarly clad but younger confederate, without taking his eyes from me.

"Be not confused," said he, "that you are an intruder here and not a guest."

With that I was led away by the confederate wearing a red fez and the guard from outside.

As we went I saw the charlady hurrying away. She had warned me but I had not heeded her. It now seemed abundantly clear to me that she had understood her employers ways very well indeed. I sat in the Library but the guard with the bright, silver sword remained vigilantly at the door.

---

[54] The Fez – a hat used widely used in the Ottoman Empire.

Suddenly the second set of doors were thrown open upon the other side of the room and two guards fairly threw Holmes in. They performed their task with so little ceremony and care that a less agile man would have fallen hard.

My friend's brows were drawn down over his keen eyes and his head was thrust forward in that way which was characteristic of him when he was out of sorts.

"I see you've met the little Turkish fellow in the red fez," said I.

"What do you make of all this nonsense?" said he, with a shake of his head.

Chapter 11 – The Dying Chieftain

"Mr. Capshaw earned his wage and warned them that the formidable specter of Mr. Sherlock Holmes was upon their trail," I answered. "They were clearly expecting us, sooner or later."

"And we arrived as soon as possible," said he.

"Where did they find you?" I asked.

"They had hounds Watson and they chased me to the trees not fifty feet inside their wall," said he, showing me a tear in his pants.

"Well I walked straight into them," I admitted, "and that little fellow told me in no uncertain terms that I was not a guest here."

"Thus freeing themselves of the burdensome tradition of hospitality," said he.

"A roughish bunch I'm thinking."

"Different people," Holmes muttered, tersely, "with different ways."

We remained under what amounted to house-arrest for another hour, then the double-doors at which Holmes had been thrown in, were opened again and in walked Freddy Capshaw himself.

"Gentlemen," he exclaimed, happily, "what a terrible thing to discover that you were little more than common criminals."

"I knocked at your front door," said I, mustering all the indignation I could, "and was clapped in here with so little civility that I now believe myself fallen among criminals."

"Well," said the young man, "there may be some truth to what you say doctor, but what am I to think of the great detective coming over a back wall and running for his very life? Had it not been for that nearby oak Mr. Holmes..."

My friend said nothing, but only stared coldly at the laughing Mr. Capshaw.

With that our captor gave the guard a casual wave of dismissal and called for us to follow.

"Let us see if we can set matters to rights for all concerned, shall we?"

ARABY

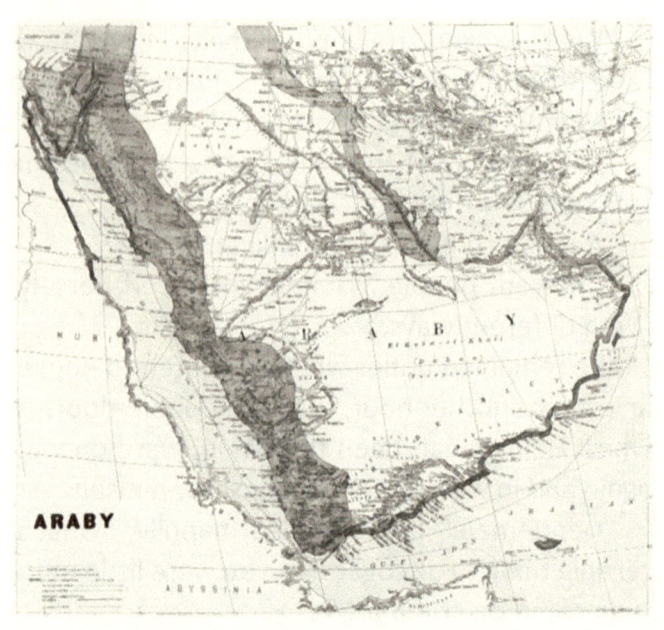

"Please do," Holmes replied, cooly.

The young man led us through the great and dazzling place filled with a vast display of exquisite furnishings, until we reached the sitting room of a bedroom suite upon an upper floor. A cheery fire burned in the grate and furniture and rugs were arranged comfortably about the room.

Here we were offered chairs near the fire and young Capshaw poured out four cups of fresh Earl Grey tea.

"Gentlemen," he said, handing us our cups as if we'd been invited to afternoon tea with the lord and lady. "You may have questions," he said, as he retrieved his own cup and took up his seat across from us.

"And you Mr. Capshaw, are the man with the answers?" Holmes asked.

"Actually no," Capshaw said, with a smile, "but he will be with us shortly."

We sat in silence for the next ten minutes while the only sound was the occasional crackle of the fire and the sipping of our tea. Neither Mr. Freddy Capshaw nor Holmes offered any conversation and I followed my friend's lead.

the door to the bedroom opened slowly and the velvet drapes covering it were parted. Then we found ourselves looking upon the very man we'd seen in the Fyldene family portrait. There could be no mistake.

He was tall, robust, and handsome, the very picture of youth and strength. I recognized him instantly as the 8-rower for the Oxford Blue.

"This is very painful," said he, in an unsteady voice, "but in that room, just there," he said, motioning behind him, "lies a man in his last hours of life. He is my father gentlemen, although we'd never met before, and I lived more than half my life without so much as dreaming of his existence. Neither of us speaks many words the other might fathom and so to communicate even our deepest feelings, we require the *intrusion* of a translator."

The young man took up his tea and sat down opposite us. Before this we'd known him only as a handsome image in photographs, but now I could see he was haggard and weary.

"This whole thing has been uncommonly hard upon me," he admitted, "and I'm not the dying man." Then looked up at us.

"As difficult as all this may have been for you," Holmes said, "can you imagine what your sudden disappearance did to your mother?"

His words were hard and unsympathetic and I could tell they were meant to shock.

"My mother?" the young man stammered.

"Yes your mother, Mrs. Elizabeth Fyldene."

"What has my mother to do with this business Mr. Holmes?" he demanded.

"You vanished without a trace," my friend said, "and yet you feign ignorance of what that would do to your mother?"

"But...I left a note for my mother, explaining everything," the young man cried out in dismay.

"Where?" Holmes demanded.

"In the very center of my desk, in my room, at Ashburn," said he, reaching into his front right pocket at the same time, almost instinctively, as if to see if he'd forgotten it after all. He pulled the liner of his pocket out to show us, empty. "I know I put it on the desk," said he, "but where could it be if she did not find it where I left it?"

"Can you really not imagine what might have become of it?" Holmes asked, searchingly.

"I left it..." he began, then he looked at Holmes. "If you are about to tell me that that devil, Fyldene, did something with it..."

> Mother. I am called away. As you know I would not engage in foolishness. I ask you to trust me without knowing the details. I will return shortly. Until then I remain your loving son, Henry

"And if he did?" Holmes asked.

"If he kept it from my mother, I'll...I'll kill him!"

"You would be too late Mr. Fyldene, for he is already dead," my friend said, shocking the young man again. "And is this the message you left your mother?"

Here Holmes produced a card bearing the "F" monogram upon the front and handed it over.

The young man opened it slowly and was struck speechless. He pulled himself up from his chair only with a herculean effort, then lurched off to the window to lean against the wall and stare across the grounds. He gripped the sides of the window frame in both hands and then he spun on his erstwhile friend, Capshaw, with clenched fists.

"You knew this and you said nothing?"

The voice of the man in the red fez came next, from behind me. He had entered quietly while the drama before us was playing out.

"You must control yourself," he commanded, in the manner of a man used to being obeyed. "Your friend had a job to do, as did I, as did we all, and that was to get you to your father before it was too late. We came around the world to see it done and we barely achieved that goal. If you think that the life or death, of this *other man* is of any significance to us, or should be to you, then you are a fool."

"But my mother?" he demanded.

"I knew nothing of that," Mr. Aydin, the man in the red fez with the bristling moustache, replied.

"And I dared not say a word," Capshaw added, "for I had no doubt you would have gone. There would've been no reasoning with you. Even Mr. Aydin could not have stopped you then."

"Your mother will not die over *this mishap*," Aydin said, cooly, "but your father will, very soon."

"I fear that is true," Henry agreed, sadly.

"And so, until then, you will remain here. You may return to your family freely, afterward."

"He is not your prisoner," I remarked, "nor is this a prison!"

The diminutive Turk turned upon me as if he still held me to be an interloper in private matters.

"That was our agreement Doctor...Watson and this young man gave us his word."

After a short pause Mr. Aydin continued.

"And he gave his dying father his word as well. What would you have the young man do now, break it? Is that what you would do Sir?"

I looked to the young Henry and he nodded in confirmation that Mr. Aydin had spoken honestly.

"No," I answered at last, "I would not have him break his vow, even to you."

"I am glad to hear it," Aydin said, glaring at me.

"This is all most easily answered," Holmes said, "simply send Dr. Watson with this note, now that we have confirmed its authenticity, and have him bring Mrs. Fyldene here to the Hermitage. She can see her son is safe, he can see that his mother is relieved, and he need never be farther than a few feet from the room where his father lies."

"Why will you not join your friend Mr. Holmes," Mr. Aydin insisted. "There is nothing more here for you gentlemen and you were never invited guests, who might make certain…presumptions or dare to give orders as you've just done?"

I also wondered why Holmes had volunteered me to go alone, but I had always been careful not to say anything which might undermine him.

"You may have gained this young man's trust Mr. Aydin," Holmes replied, civilly, "although by what mean you accomplished it I will not hazard. Be assured, however, that you have not earned mine and having now found him, you may be sure that I will not leave here without him. Such was *my vow* to his mother."

"And knowing that my mother has indeed commissioned these gentlemen," Henry insisted, "you must now consider them my personal guests here and treat them in accordance hereafter."

The young Henry spoke as a man who was not going to be denied. "As for this Capshaw fellow, on the other hand, I have no use at all for him and no desire to see his face here even for another minute. I demand his removal."

Capshaw looked to his employer with pleading eyes, but a simple nod was enough to send him on his way. In short order he and I were delivered to the station in the same carriage, but it being a short trip we shared no further conversation.

At the station and upon Holmes' instructions, I sent telegrams to Mrs. Fyldene, Lestrade, and Redgrave. I told them that Henry had been found safe and alive and explained the waylaying of the note. It was now a closed case.

I gave few details and told Mrs. Fyldene that I'd soon be with her. I would serve as her escort so that she could soon look upon her son.

As for Mr. Freddy Capshaw, neither Holmes nor I ever saw the man again.

I found Mrs. Fyldene more radiant than ever and full of relief and anticipation at seeing her son.

She was also near the end of her strength and I wondered if she had even eaten or slept during all the time he had been missing.

When she rose to greet me the poor woman suddenly fainted and would have collapsed to the floor had I not caught her. I saw her to a settee and plied her with a couple sips of brandy and water before she began to recover.

"When was the last time you ate?" I asked.

"I fear I haven't...I'm not sure," she confessed, then she collapsed upon my shoulder and began weeping.

I gave her my handkerchief and she continued on for several minutes before she had exhausted herself.

"I must apologize," she said, as she collected herself.

"I will not hear of it," I said. "You have pushed yourself beyond the limits of endurance and now you suffer the consequences Mrs. Fyldene."

"You have given me back my son," she sighed.

"It was Mr. Holmes," I insisted.

"Yes, of course," she agreed, laying her head back down upon my shoulder, "but he could not have done it without you, "she whispered. "You have a heroic soul Dr. Watson."

We arrived at the Station in the afternoon and though it was but a short walk and I had insisted that the poor woman eat something before we left, I hailed a cab outside the depot.

We were met at the door not by the bedecked Saracen with the fearful sword but by Holmes and Mr. Aydin, standing side by side but clearly still not upon amicable terms.

"Mr. Holmes!" she cried as she rushed up to the door and flung her arms about my friend. "You've done it! You've done the impossible!"

"It is true that your son is alive and safe Mrs. Fyldene," said he, cautioning, "but you must save your happiness for him, as he has had a most trying time of it himself."

"Dr. Watson showed me the note and said all would be explained."

"And young Henry is the one to answer all your questions, I assure you. Now, this gentleman is Mr. Aydin, he is in charge here and has watched over your son since he disappeared."

"My agreement was for you to be informed," Aydin said in self-defense.

"I understand very well that it was the final act of spite by my late husband," Mrs. Fyldene said, full of understanding. "So rest assured Mr. Aydin that I bear you nothing but good will."

The reunion of mother and son took place in the sitting room near the dying man, by which I took it that there had been no improvement in his condition.

"I had no idea when I departed," Henry began to explain, "that my message would be waylaid by that, that devil Fyldene and that you would suffer such apprehensions."

"All is forgotten now that I find you safe."

"My true father lies in the next room," he said, in a voice weak with emotion.

"Then you've met."

"He is near his sad end mother and is all alone in the world. How I came to be mixed up in all of this, to have this part in such a mystery, even now I have no words to describe it."

"It was love my son, all love. A reckless, selfish love I see now, but what is love if not the threat of shipwreck and doom?"

"I still don't understand," he stuttered, very much like he must have as a boy I thought.

"It is very simple son," Mrs. Fyldene replied, "the only answer to all of this, to you in fact, was the love your father and I felt for each other."

"Some would consider it madness," she said, "and perhaps we were mad, mad to dream of a world where we could be together, with you, and be at peace, but it was love. I am sorry that it has made your young life such a misery. You were innocent, always innocent, and should not have had to face a bitter existence with a man like Henry Fyldene."

"Fyldene is gone now," young Henry said, "and if I never hear his name again I will be a happy man. My true father had this drawing of you and through his translator he told me it was the only image he ever had."

"We each had such an image of the other."

"Then you have one of him?" Henry asked.

"Here it is," she said, pulling the image from her pocket. "I've kept it all these years."

"Then this is the first time these images have been together since..."

"Since we left Ottoman Arabia, when you were a baby," she said, "but has he told you why he came to England?"

"He said he became the chief of his tribe and had many fine sons. They were handsome and brave, but his people have been at war for a great many lifetimes. Now I am the only son he has left mother. I am his firstborn and his last surviving son and his wish was to see me before he died."

"Oh Henry," she said, nearly overcome.

"He'd love to see you one last time mother, I know he would. He has little time left, perhaps no more than an hour."

"Dare we see each other again, after...all this time my son?"

"A farewell between two who have loved so deeply seems only right to me," said he, "and as you are my parents..."

"Yes that settles it then," she said, standing up. "Will you take me to him?"

They made their way nervously through the curtained doorway and into the bedroom, while Holmes and I watched from the door.

The man wore a snow-white turban and though only a shadow of the young man was recognizable in the hardened face before us, I could see that he had been a fierce warrior once.

Upon seeing the woman he had loved he called out and Mr. Aydin and a nurse helped him sit up. They said nothing, but embraced in silence for several minutes, their heads upon each other's shoulders, tears, and smiles.

After this the Bedouin chieftain laid back upon his pillows and they looked into each other's eyes and held hands.

Holmes and I withdrew to the fire in the sitting room and spoke quietly together.

"Where did you find the note?" I asked, for the whole thing had puzzled me to no end.

"At the House of Death," he whispered, "not a foot from the dead man's hand."

"Then you could have told Mrs. Fyldene."

"A few hours earlier? Perhaps, but I had not verified the note and after everything she'd gone through I was unwilling to risk it for a few hours. The devil knew what he was doing when he took the note Watson. There was a cold and evil heart in that man and it is a chilling reminder."

"A reminder of what?" I asked.

"Of how many people there are in our world who, though we may pass them upon the street, see them in business, or mix with them in society, are true devils simply biding their time and looking for the chance to do evil and cause suffering."

"That is a bleak insight indeed," I admitted.

"Bleak and dark," said he, closing his eyes in meditation, "and yet absolutely true."

An hour passed by before Mrs. Fyldene and her son returned to the sitting room and joined us by the fire.

"He is gone now," the young man said.

"But we cannot thank you enough gentlemen, for making this final meeting possible. You are a marvel Mr. Holmes."

J. B. Varney

Chapter 12 – Darlington

In gratitude for our service to them the New Year brought us an invitation to visit Darlington.

"I suppose we must go," Holmes remarked, as he dropped the note upon the table.

"You act as if you've been drafted into some unsavory business instead of a few days in one of the country's finest homes."

"It isn't that Watson," Holmes reasoned, "I am in the middle of a chemical experiment which may very well rewrite the science of adhesives."

"Adhesives?" I stuttered, in disbelief.

My friend just stared at me as if I were a newly discovered species, wholly separate from Homo Sapiens. Perhaps Homo Watsonensis or the like .

"You must just make the best of it," I insisted. "After all, I wouldn't think that wearing a tuxedo and eating the fine food in England could be too much of a burden for you."

"For a few days then," he considered.

"It is a gesture Holmes," I said, "of the sincerest appreciation, for the returning of her son."

"Have you forgotten the check she gave us? That was a very clear *gesture* and it had a finality to it did it not? You deposited it after all."

"Yes well, there is that, but this is considered a proper public demonstration of that thanks."

He stared at me a little longer.

"I do understand the obligations of society," Holmes replied, "I simply do not always agree with them my good fellow."

That was really what was at issue. Holmes was in many ways a puzzle even to himself. That he was the master of solving puzzles and mysteries was, in consideration of this fact, a true wonder.

"You'll just have to make the best of it," I said.

Our invitation also contained the message from Mrs. Fyldene that she and her sons had, after much consideration, chosen to take her maiden name for their surname. So the former Henry Fyldene, the Younger, now simply became Henry Osborne and his mother was once more returned to Elizabeth Osborne.

On our first morning in the palatial residence we came down to breakfast to find the house in a tumult. Two maids passed us without concern, weeping. A footman stood leaning upon a marble pillar, staring at the ground, and upon entering the dining room we found even those few who sat at table were not eating.

"What is it?" Holmes asked Henry.

"It is *this* Mr. Holmes. *It* has happened!" With that the young man pointed his finger into the headline of the paper.

"The Death of Gordon – Terrible Massacres in Khartoum," Holmes whispered, so as not to upset the others more than they already were. "Women and children were not spared."

Henry Fyldene

"Seven thousand killed, the garrison wiped out, Gordon killed upon the steps of the palace, and the Mahdi reestablishes slavery."

"They fell just days before the relief column arrived," the grandfather growled angrily from the head of the table, "Two days!"

"Just two days!" I repeated, in shock.

I'd seen war and battles and I knew how close such things could come, but a war upon women and children, and open massacres, such things didn't set well with me.

"I can't imagine an entire nation feeling as I now do," Henry said, almost to himself.

"Gordon, his soldiers, and every man in the city, they were all slaughtered," Henry's half-brother Alfred said, his eyes red with welling tears.

After breakfast when we found ourselves left alone, I looked at my friend.

"You were right Holmes," I said. "I didn't want to believe that they would be abandoned by the Prime Minister, but you knew. You said they'd be slaughtered, thousands, even the civilians."

"What you may not understand Watson, is that I didn't want to be right," Holmes sighed. "I would gladly have been proven wrong upon the point."

"But you knew, two months ago, you knew and you were right!"

"I'm sorry to say Watson, that being right in such matters often only requires that one be honest."

Henry Fyldene

"Honest?" I stammered.

"Yes my friend. There really is nothing new under the sun which has not been done before. This case, with all it facets, was a rare exception, but the rulers of empires and kingdoms have been abandoning and sacrificing their faithful leaders and brave soldiers upon the altar of convenience and corruption for ages past. If we know history then all that is required is to be honest, then we can recognize the age-old signs when we see them anew. Sadly, it is a small thing to predict the fate of all of the Gordons and Khartoum's as they come. It is even a small enough thing to expect that such atrocities will still be happening in a hundred and a thousand should mankind stumble on that long."

"This was a crime," I muttered, angrily.

"Yes it was my good fellow but if you think those in power will pay, then you have mistaken the law for something it isn't."

"You've spoken of the difference between the law and justice before," I said, "but until now I had never felt how unjust the law can be."

"The law is relative," said he, matter-of-factly, "and those in power oversee it. The corrupt walk free while they work to shackle their enemies under the law. However Watson, justice is truly blind. By definition justice can see no difference between the great and small."

"And that is why you work for justice."

Henry Fyldene

"I represent justice so far as my feeble powers go," said he, "but let us change the subject to something less painful."

"What do you have in mind?" I asked.

"If you would look at the top of page three of the Times," he said, pointing, "yes, just there."

"British Museum to gain Nineveh Collection," I read aloud. "What is this Holmes?"

"A vast collection of archeological treasures was found Watson but read on."

"Laughton Hall?" I exclaimed, as I continued. "Sir Malcolm Caldor-Vaughn?" I said. "Can it be?"

"He served as a diplomat in Ottoman Arabia before his time in Parliament."

"Yes, but how could he have been hidden so great a treasure in a private residence in London without the world knowing?" I asked. "Where was it hidden?"

"Do you recall how you were discovered on the night we burgled the Hall, but I was not?"

I thought back to that night.

"Yes," I said, "I recall you found a secret stair or something, wasn't it? And you hid there while the residence was searched."

"I found the doorway during my examination of Sir Malcolm's study and I hid there when the alarm was raised," he continued. "You fled into the night, but I descended the stair, which has since been confirmed to have been laid down in Ancient Roman times."

Henry Fyldene

"And that was where Sir Malcolm hid this vast collection?"

"A truly impressive collection as you will find out later this year when they open to the public."

"You informed the authorities," I said, realizing what my friend had been driving at all along.

"Just so and if the family is to be believed, none of them knew anything about it."

"This case," I remarked, "it has been...unique."

"And just when I'd begun to wonder about London's criminals," Holmes said.

At that moment the lovely Elizabeth Osborne, looking more beautiful than ever, leaned in at the door and smiled at us.

"I don't suppose you gentlemen would care to escort our party to the Savoy Theatre tonight. Gilbert and Sullivan's new show, 'The Mikado,' is opening and we could do with some cheering up. It promises to be a rare treat and we'll meet Cousin Alfred and Maria there as well, then go to Mancini's afterward."[55]

---

[55] Gilbert and Sullivan's "Mikado" would run for almost 700 performances. The Alfred and Maria referred to by Elizabeth Osborne were Prince Alfred and Princess Maria, the Duke and Duchess of Edinburgh.

The End

Thank you for reading:

The Disappearance of Henry Fyldene

Sherlock Holmes
The Dowager Baroness

A Sherlock Holmes Resurgent Mystery

J. B. Varney

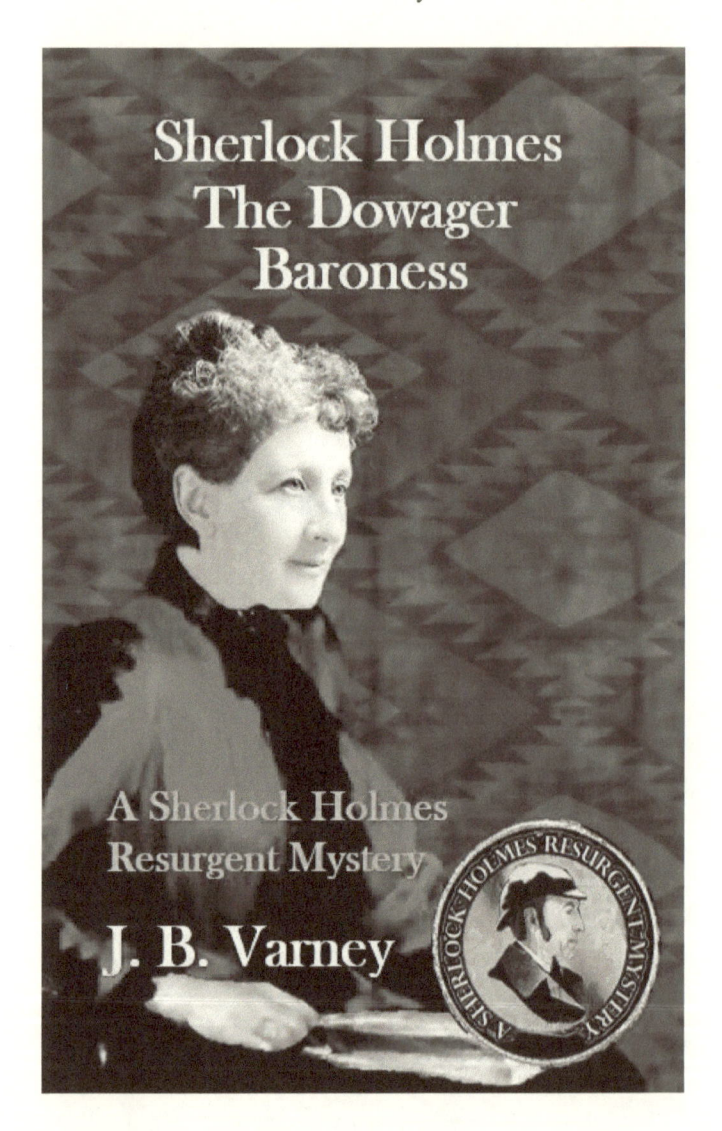

The Dowager Baroness
coming soon

What's next for Holmes & Watson?

In the summer of 1885 a London businessman appeared at 221B Baker Street and unburdened himself of certain suspicions. "Please tell me I'm seeing evil where there is none for I am at my wits end Mr. Holmes."

The person at the center of the man's suspicions was the diminutive Lady Cecily Ingham, née de la Haye, the Right Honorable Dowager Baroness of Mortmain and widow of the adventurer Sir Clarence Ingham. A partner in her husband's travels she'd completed a storm-tossed circumnavigation of the globe which included wintering in a native winter camp on the Plains and crossing the Sierra Nevada mountains. She now held court from her palatial home near Canterbury, where the highborn heiress with a common touch had cultivated relationships far and wide as well as high and low.

"The female is the most deadly of the species Mr. Holmes," she said, over an exceptional Darjeeling.

"She is either exactly what she appears Watson, or she is the most cunning architect of evil we've thus encountered."

Holmes had his doubts at first, but the woman drew him into one of the most chilling cases in our long career.

"Come Watson, the game is afoot!"

The Game is...still afoot!

J. B. Varney

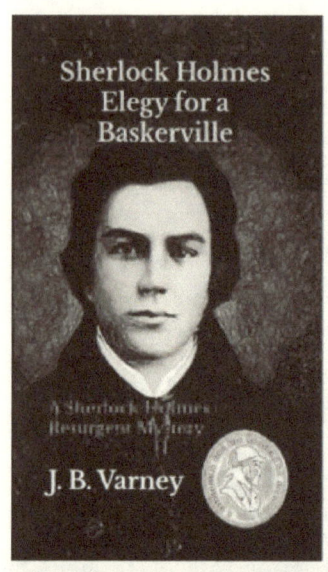

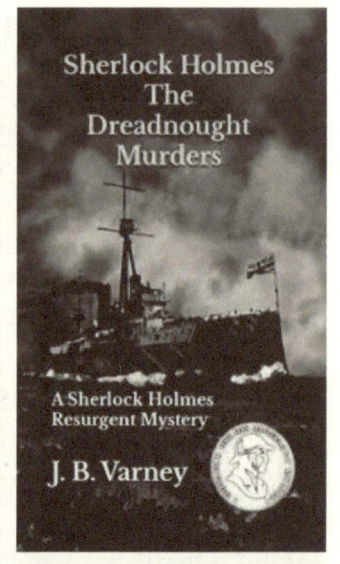

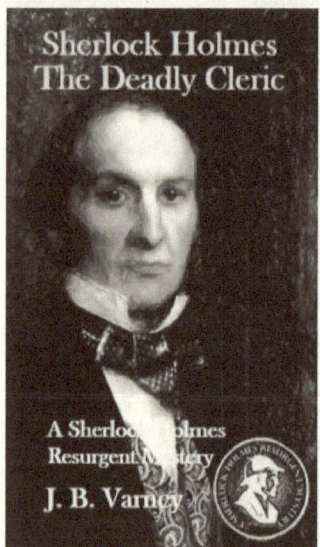

The Resurgent Mysteries

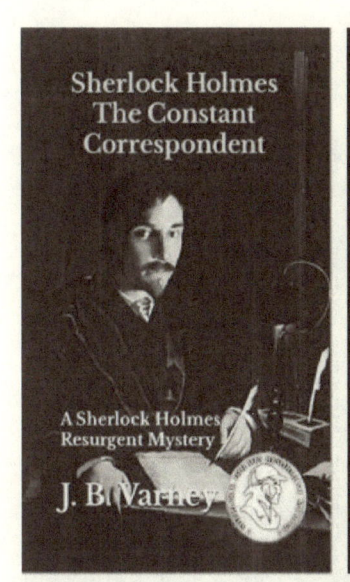

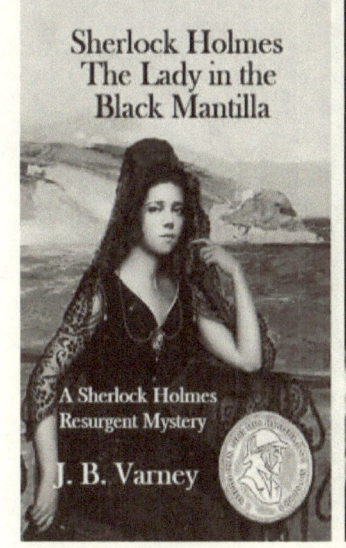

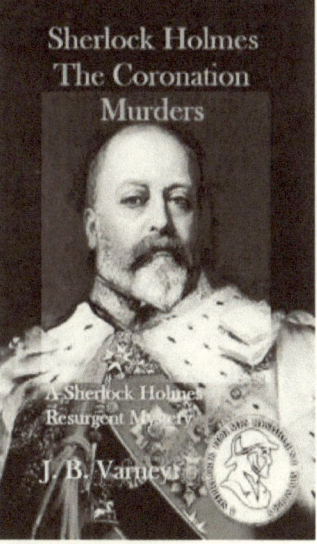

Henry Fyldene

The Resurgent Mysteries

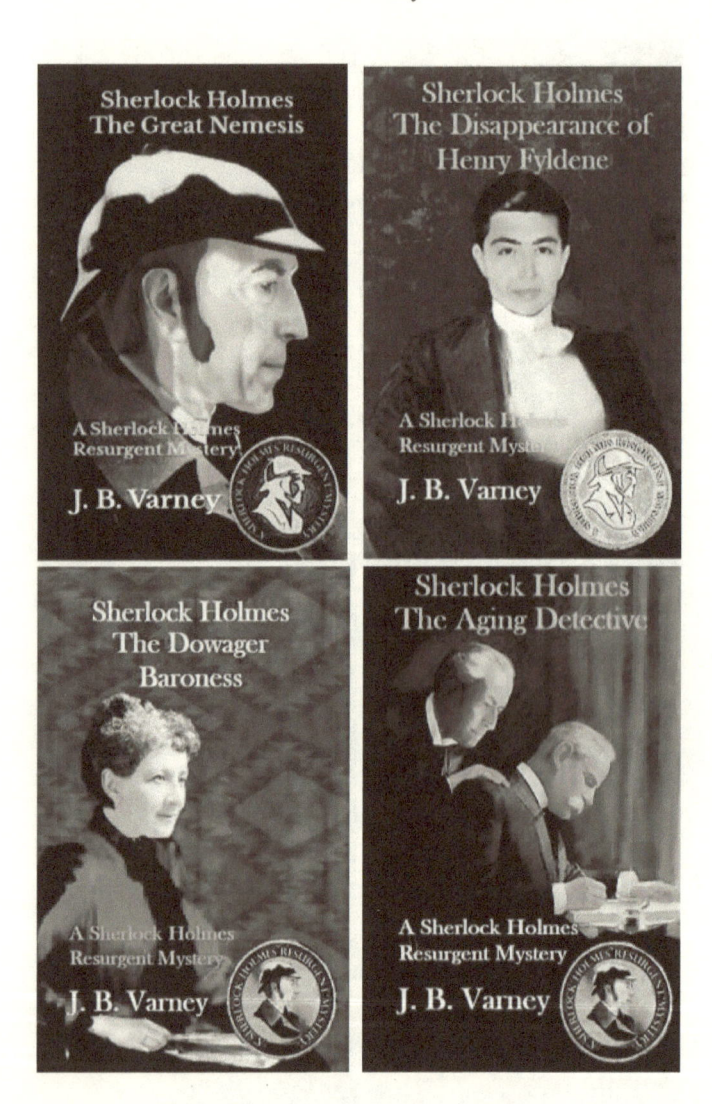

**The Dowager Baroness
& The Aging Detective
coming soon**

ABOUT THE AUTHOR

J. B. Varney "discovered" Sherlock Holmes as a boy. It was a time when none of his peers had read even one of Sir Arthur Conan Doyle's mysteries and thus began his life-long love of mystery and twisting plots.

Mr. Varney is a historian, genealogist, and descendant of many of the ancient families of Europe whose names grace the pages of his Resurgent Mysteries.

The game is...still afoot!"

Made in United States
Troutdale, OR
04/22/2025